RAMBLING WITH AN ELUSIVE DOVE

RAMBLING WITH AN ELUSIVE DOVE

Theresa W. Glover

For — Gregory and Eileen Westley,
Hugs and smiles: life's Health foods!
Enjoy !
Theresa W. Glover
July 14, 2004

Writer's Showcase
New York Lincoln Shanghai

Rambling with an Elusive Dove

Writer's Showcase
an imprint of iUniverse, Inc.

For information address:
iUniverse, Inc.
2021 Pine Lake Road, Suite 100
Lincoln, NE 68512
www.iuniverse.com

ISBN: 0-595-25824-7

Printed in the United States of America

Contents

▼

CHAPTER 1

▼

LEANNA'S BACKGROUND

"No! She didn't ask! She just upped and moved herself right into my home! I should have looked at more than one possible reason why. But, I'm a mother, and my heart had gone out to her as the underdog in her marital relationship. Ha! Maybe one of these days I'll learn."

I guess I need to explain about this dilemma that I have found myself in.

The big gold chair in the living room is where I sit much of the time when I'm inside. I had just seated myself there when I heard Racina.

"Hi, Mama. How you doin'? Sure is a beautiful day for sitting on the porch. Have you been outside watching the world go by?"

"Hi, honey. I just a few minutes ago came in to sit. The sun had gotten me a little too hot. I do love sitting on my porch, you know, 'cause it's part of my house, and I love all of my house. How was your day?"

"Oh, I can't complain. Nothing exciting happened that doesn't happen almost every day. We did have some squirmy visitors from the Jason Elementary School. They were fourth graders. You know, I'm not so sure introducing children to investment operations this early in life is beneficial to them. But, I suppose it does give them some ideas about the various kinds of businesses that make the world go round. So, what'cha been doing all day?"

"Not much. Just the usual kinds of things."

"Like?"

"Like thinking about some of the people who usually walk past here dressed to the nines. You know, when I was a child, the clothes people wore were artistic designs. Not today. Designs and patterns appear to be drastically thrown together, exhibiting little, if any, artistic beauty. I think I'll go shopping tomorrow, I need a new outfit."

"Mama, you have more outfits now than you can fit into your closets. You don't need anything else! You just *want* a new outfit."

"I need one, I want one, and I'm gonna buy one." I figured it was time I left that room. I headed for the kitchen. "What'cha want to drink with your supper? I have fresh lemonade, iced sun tea, and cold water, of course. I'll bet you don't drink any water during the day, do you?"

"Who likes the taste of water, blah! I'll have iced tea. What's for supper, anyway?"

"Oh, something good to eat. You know. Food." I'm serious and start laughing heartily as I disappear into the kitchen. I catch her off guard every time I say those same words.

Racina, always quite headstrong, bristles at any conversation she feels is leaning toward or encroaching upon her private life. Sometimes we get caught up in heated discussions that turn ugly and regrettable. Regrettable for me because I do not need to have my every word disputed. This was one day I refused to be suckered into even a slight disagreement with Racina, or anyone.

Racina followed close behind me to the kitchen so that she could set the table for our early evening meal. That day our plates were ladened with buttered yams, turnip greens with diced turnips, and meatloaf. Every meal in my home was served with some kind of hot bread, and tonight's bread was hot cornbread.

We talked trivially now, and Racina spoke of the office rumor about changes to be made on her job.

"Some man from out in Utah is being coaxed to come here and set up his method of actuarial practices. Rumor has it that the bosses think his method will increase our net finances by fifteen percent the first year he is employed. That might be great if any of the home employees ever get to see an increase in their monthly salaries as a result."

As soon as our supper was over, Racina left the table, walked into the living room, sat down in my gold recliner and fell sound asleep. I didn't mind having to do the dishes alone every day. It was my house and I did as I pleased, when I pleased, and however I pleased.

For a long while I felt I had figured out why Racina's naps were usually two to three hours long, so I kept very quiet so as not to disturb her. And I was right, her "domestic tranquillity" hadn't been tranquil for sometime. Nightly, it was about nine-thirty or ten o'clock when Racina left my home and went to her own. None of my children believed I was wise enough to figure that they might be covering up something about their marital relationships.

Next day, as soon as I finished breakfast, I called Chamia and Gracie and convinced them to join me on a shopping spree. We met, shopped, and then I treated them to lunch. You bet I bought myself something, a blue suit that Chamia and Gracie said looked exactly like the one I wore three Sundays ago. I knew Racina would have a criticism.

You know, I'm not so dumb. I've now been living alone for a little more than a year. But all of the children think I should not be living alone, not at this time in my life. I'm aware that Racina is here every day; Larson, once or twice a week; and Neva, every other day. Many of the grandchildren who are old enough to understand believe that I need them around me so they also make regular visits.

When I don't openly welcome my brood, they feel I am unappreciative of their concern. Truly, I'm happy that they think so highly of me that they want to be near, but, gosh, I can do without all of their questions. "Mom, did you remember to lock both doors? Are you sure you turned off all the burners after you made your hot chocolate, or hot tea, or whatever it was you made hot tonight?" Yet, they go on and on, even after I have assured them that I'm all right. I tell them, "Trust me, I'm all right."

CHAPTER 2

▼

HOME, ETC.

A kaleidoscopic sunbeam penetrating the front window pane is flooding my face with its warmth. I know I am not nearly the same weight that I maintained through the years of being married to Darden, and my children won't let me forget it even though I decline to view myself in the mirror. My hair is all silver, now, and I usually wear it pulled into a loose ball pinned on top of my head. All of the children attribute my weight loss to the aging and grieving processes.

You see, my Darden died a few months back, and my children all think I won't be long behind him, especially since we were married for nearly seventy years. I suppose the children think they see or sense great emotion in my unusual silence about Darden's death, but I am, in my own way, still thanking him for having provided me with a well-maintained and mortgage-free home.

All of this intense attention that my children, and grandchildren, are now heaping upon me is beginning to stiffle my very existence to the point where I don't always seem to be able to think rationally for myself about much of anything.

At the age of eighty-five years young, I know I'm healthy. I've always tried to keep myself physically, mentally, and morally fit by faithfully doing the same kinds of things I prescribed for myself years ago.

On one particular day, I got angry with two of my children because they criticized me about *my* housekeeping. I left their presence and found my way to my gold chair situated just to the right of the front door. I sat poised on my left buttock, with my right leg crossed high up and heavy over my left thigh. I began humming a song I had heard one of them singing, and found myself swinging and bouncing my crossed leg. Suddenly a bevy of thoughts flooded my mind. I frowned. I got frustrated when I was not able to slow down nor sort my thoughts. I remember swinging my right leg downward, and stamping my foot to the floor. I left the room and went out onto the front porch. I sat down in my blue caned-bottom rocking chair and began rocking. Within minutes, my rocking torpedoed me back to Cayuga where I was born.

No matter what time of the day, when I sit in my blue rocking chair on the front porch, it's like I can feel Darden's arms around me giving me a gentle bear hug. It is as if he knows that I need him at a particular moment, and suddenly he's right there. Memories of my Darden are all that I have now, and those memories soothe my anger. I close my eyes and allow the past to take over my mind.

My family lived in a two-story white frame house surrounded by a two-foot high white wooden fence. The house was located in the 300 block of East LeHigh Street. I didn't want for friends to play with. I already had two older brothers, one older sister, and one younger brother with whom I could play. But I played mostly with the other children who lived on our block.

The Browns, an elderly couple with no children, lived just to the left of us. The Beckers and their five children were next door to the Browns. Just past them lived the young couple named Jayson and their newborn son. On the other side of my family's house, and three houses down, lived the Sawyers. They were a childless couple and really didn't want to have social contact with anyone in our block. No one on the block cared, as long as they weren't insulting to us neighborhood children with their antisocial attitude. The Ledbetters, two doors away, had three children, and the Poussants and their daughter were next door to the right. The children of the families in that one block all got along very well.

Most mornings, shortly after sunrise, my brothers and I and my sister, one right after the other, hit the floor hard to be the first one in the bathroom and then to be ready to go downstairs to breakfast. Mama said the sounds of our feet hitting the floor was audible down to the kitchen and that's how she knew to hurry breakfast along. It didn't take us children long to wash and dress and bound down the stairs.

As soon as we children got seated at the kitchen table, Mama would ask, "So who wants biscuits with breakfast today?"

"I do, Mama." I *always* answered first.

"Me, too, Mama," beamed Mitchell, next.

My older siblings seldom answered Mama and took whatever Mama offered for our meals. Just as surely as a day was sunny and our breakfast was finished, we'd ask Mama to be excused from the table.

Many mornings Mama would hear a faint rap on our kitchen door and knew that it was Macy Becker come to get me, her favorite playmate, to come out to play. Macy's little sister, Shana, sometimes would be there with Macy and the three of us would race from my house to Mrs. Ledbetter's house to call out Nettie and Lillian for play. It was seldom long before Amelia Poussant joined with us, and soon afterwards Sophia and Carolyn Cousoots came over from across the street. We even had fun deciding in whose yard we wanted to play.

No matter whose yard we chose as the play area, we almost always played "house," and our first concern was cooking. Amelia usually brought her baby doll and carriage to play, so she always volunteered to "go to the store" for food. Our "store" was any place in any one of our yards.

Sometimes we used dandelion leaves and flowers, clover flower buds and leaves, wild strawberries and blackberries, and whatever weeds and fruits that grew in our yards that we thought looked enough like the foods our mothers cooked. Sometimes, one of our mothers would offer us a leaf or two of collards, turnip greens, or some other leafy vegetable while pretending to be the "store owner" for a day. We often took hours to prepare our "meals," then we'd feed our straw dolls that our mothers had made for us. Only Amelia had a store bought doll.

"My baby had the colic last night so I called the doctor," Amelia said as she began to feed her doll.

"So what did the doctor say to do, Amy?" Amy was the name we always called her.

"Oh, he said I have nothing to worry over, that Missy will be right once I give her a dose of castor oil."

And so our play continued with us mimicking our mothers' words and actions in our game of "house."

I must have been about four years old when I became real serious about my "cooking," and I occasionally "baked" desserts for my father. After my family was finished eating the main course of our supper meal, I would go fetch the dessert I had made for my daddy and put it on the table right by his left elbow. I sat to the left of him, always.

"Today I made your bestest dessert, Daddy, it's peach cobbler."

"Oh, honey, how sweet of you. But I don't think I can eat another thing for right now. Maybe later tonight if I get hungry I'll have some."

"Okay, Daddy, but don't eat it all up. I made nuff for Mama, too."

"Sure, honey, I understand. I'll share it with Mama."

Always, when the next morning dawned and I saw my clean dessert dishes, I believed my parents had enjoyed my cooking. I was some proud!

Of course, I would be all of six and one-half years before I realized that I had been pushing my daddy into some serious thinking stages every time I put my "cooking" at his elbow. He did tell me several years later, "Whew, sometimes I didn't know if I could think fast enough. I certainly didn't want to ever hurt your feelings about your cooking."

Sometimes even the boys in the neighborhood joined in the "house" play with us girls. The boys worked outside the home and brought home their paychecks of green tree leaves or pieces of paper they had gotten from their mothers. They didn't know how to count, but they pretended. At ages three to seven years old, no one of us knew much about anything.

My rocking must have slowed, for not much more came to mind about the years before I began kindergarten. I did remember that sometimes I would fall asleep on the floor when I was too tired to climb onto my bed for my midday nap. And when I awoke I would be on a folded quilt that either my mother or my sister Zeena had rolled me onto to get me off the bare floor.

My sister Zeena was some eight years older than myself. And though she didn't share play with me, she did occasionally offer me suggestions on what and how to play certain games. She even took time, often, to tell or read stories to me. I truly adored my big sister.

A car backfired as it neared my house which startled me into fast rocking. Then, I was remembering that me and Delia, my cousin, also played together daily. Many times Delia would take her noon nap at my house, and vice versa if I was at her house. Also, almost daily, she and I got into a fuss before being called home. We argued mostly over a game of jackrocks. We used small coal embers and pea-size gravel for our rocks. We used a small rubber ball that we took from a wooden paddle and used it for our toss-up missile in our jackrocks games. Some days, Delia got picky about how high in the air the ball was to be tossed when I had to gather all ten of the jacks at once. That would set on my bottom nerve about as heavy as a leg-filled cowboy boot that had accidentally landed on someone's foot.

I had several cousins right there in Cayuga, and we were all nearly the same age. When they came to my house, we mostly played chase games. We all loved to run. My Mama said she and her sisters would be completely exhausted from watching us running, even though they would just be sitting and talking with each other.

I was nearly seven years of age when my family suffered an unusual financial situation. My daddy was a dock worker at the Succhor River Marine Basin. He had never been absent nor tardy in all of his adult years working there. He was known as "Mr. Dependable." But one particular year was not to be in my daddy's favor.

First, he got sick with the flu. Mama told her sister, Nazarea, "That stuff gripped him like a vise holding two steel bars in place." Though Daddy got over the flu, it was one month later that he got sick with pneumonia. About that, Mama revealed to Aunt Nazarea, "The flu enfeebled his legs because his gait was wobbly. But that pneumonia made him puke every hour. He developed a hacking cough trying to clear his lungs. He needed so much pure oxygen. Those two sicknesses nearly killed him." It took my daddy almost a year to be well enough to return to work.

In the meantime, during Daddy's sickness, Mama had to work away from home to earn money to help pay house bills. She couldn't really earn much because she only knew how to be a housekeeper, a job which paid minimum wages. I have to tell you, though, Mama may have had little academic schooling, but she sure was laced throughout with intelligence—the common sense kind!

My two older brothers, Charles and Jarrett, and my sister, Zeena, were of legal age to work for wages, so they each found paying jobs and contributed their pay to help with household expenses. At the turn of the twentieth century there wasn't this great concern about everyone getting a good education. Instead, if help was needed to put food on the table, then help is what was expected of you.

Charles and Jarrett got hired down at Mr. Chutney's Clothes Factory. Their work meant standing all day. Zeena didn't want that. She got a job at the neighborhood laundry/cleaners, tagging and sorting soiled clothes.

Mama had a brother named Norris who had been married to Mavis King for seventeen years. They didn't have any children. They asked Mama and Daddy if I could come live with them. I heard them say they hoped their offer was not received as derogatory in any way. I learned much, much later that the pompous Aunt Mavis had eyed me as being a little ragamuffin, yet quite beautiful. In other words, Aunt Mavis did not believe in allowing any child to play until it appeared the child's clothes or body could ever become clean. Aunt Mavis secretly wanted to turn me into a young lady of elegance. *That* was the true bent of Aunt Mavis's concern.

There is that big moving truck passing through here again. I wonder if anyone of my neighbors is moving out. I haven't heard any scuttlebutt. Ha, there is a strange dark green Ford car following slowly behind it. Maybe both the driver of that truck and the driver of the car are not on the right street. I'm sure I would have heard from someone if any of my neighbors were moving out. After some twenty minutes of asking and not being able to give answer to my own questions, I cranked up my rocking again, and yes, my thoughts of yesteryear's Cayuga returned.

Uncle Norris and Aunt Mavis lived in a huge two-story brown house. The size of it was awesome to me. The front yard stretched some 150 feet wide and about 200 feet deep. I figured their house to be about twenty-three blocks away. That was like being in another city to me. I thought they must be kinda rich based on the size of their house and the pretty clothes they wore.

When I first moved to their house I really believed I must be in or near heaven because they just seemed to give me almost anything they thought I might have wanted. They dressed me in real fancy clothes, you know, like lace-trimmed dresses, with lace-trimmed sox to match, and patent-leather shoes. Even my underclothes had lace on them. But mainly I got to have as much ice cream as I could eat without getting sick, not to mention as much of my favorite peanut butter log candy as my stomach would take. With all that stuff being showered on me, it was some time before I began to miss my sisters and brothers, and my Mom and Dad.

Little did I know, but in less than six weeks, I began to not have to put on my Sunday-go-to-meeting frocks since I was just going to loll around the house, having stories read to me, or some such thing. I was with Aunt Mavis twenty-four hours every day since she was a stay-at-home wife. Uncle Norris worked so I got to see him only after five o'clock every weekday afternoon.

It took little more than a month of living with them before I began to pester Aunt Mavis about when I was gonna see my family. Now that the supply of ice cream and candy had gotten less frequent, I guess I started to feel sorry for myself. I started to wonder why I was chosen to be the one away from my family, why I had to miss seeing everybody. "Aunt Mavis, can we go see Mama, today?" I would ask about three times in a week. Hours extended into days into weeks into almost a month longer, and I did not get to see my siblings nor my cousin Delia. I sorely missed Delia's fussing. I was now aware of not really playing except when I was at school. Most of the time Aunt Mavis wanted me to find a book to read. Oh, she had lots of children's books that she thought I should be able to read.

Over a short course of time I learned that my older sister and brothers frolicked twice weekly at the Succhor River Wharf, a favorite hangout for teenagers. It was open Friday and Saturday afternoons and evenings. There, the teenagers danced to the music playing on the coin-in-the-slot phonograph. Or, they sat at tables and in booths, and filled their stomachs with fried oysters, clams, and crabs. Deep-fried salted mullets were everyone's favorite. All of six times during my first year away from home, Charles, Jarrett, and Zeena took me with them to the Wharf. After that year, it seemed they just forgot about me.

I favored the Wharf for one reason only—for the crab meat sandwiches. You might not believe it, but I had to be told when enough was enough of the crab meat. Once, in fact, I ate so much of it that I heaved and retched all the way home, and well into the night. Cramps gripped my stomach. I pleaded with Aunt Mavis, "I don't want to take that stuff. Mama would never give me castor oil. It ain't gonna cure nothing anyhow. I'm gonna tell on you! Please, Aunt Mavis." The cramps gnarled in and gripped my stomach all through the night.

Oh, the crab meat and all of the seafood was fresh daily, so it was concluded that I had simply eaten too much. Everybody but me, Leanna Mallard, knew that fact. They talked about that fact and included, "She's addicted." I was a mature woman before I understood a definition for the word "addicted" with reference to me and crab meat.

My older brothers and sister had another reason for having me tag along with them to the Wharf. They were trying to help relax my fear of the river. Oh, no, not to swim in the river. Not one of them did. They wanted me to realize that I could walk along the banks of the river and the river would stay where it belonged.

But I was terrified of the river. Every time I dared to look at it, I saw it buck like an untamed horse newly pent in a corral. Next, it became a snake, slithering alongside the bank, trying to strike the ground wherever I dared to walk. It was very difficult for me to separate the reality from my thoughts, and often my thoughts of what the river could do to me actually made me dizzy. I would faint every time they coaxed me close to the riverbank.

"Oh, God, why am I shaking so? Lord, Lord, my thoughts are controlling me! Right now, this moment, I can hear the rush of the water of that great river. Lord, if I sink any lower in this chair I'll wind up on the porch. Help me, Lord, take these thoughts out of my head."

Abruptly, my rocking stopped, my thoughts had me afraid that I would rock too far forward and right into that great river. The screams and actions of happiness by the little girl across the street playing on her tricycle attracted my attention. I must have stared at her for ten minutes.

Minutes later, when I felt quite calm, I began rocking again. Yes, my rocking took me into my past again, but thankfully, I did not then return to the Succhor River.

"Leanna. Leanna, honey, come here please."

Yes, I heard Aunt Mavis calling me, but I didn't want to answer her right then because I was not where I was supposed to be. I was away from the fence and sitting on the curb. There I could better watch all the neighborhood children playing. I think they would play nearest my aunt and uncle's house so that I could come play with them. They never really asked me, but that's the way children played. They were shy and supposed you were shy also, so if they played nearby, no one had to be asked with words, you just knew that it was alright to join in.

Someone had found a well-used tennis ball, or maybe it was a deflated red rubber ball. Someone else had picked up a tree limb. It was about a foot and a half to two feet long. Each child took a turn and swatted at the ball. The tree limb, if it connected with the ball, knocked the ball distances past the children. The hitter would run furiously from one spot to another spot. The hitter would be "out" if tagged by the person who picked up the ball. They called their game Stickball.

Like I said, I heard Aunt Mavis calling me, but I sure wanted to get into that Stickball game, so for the moment I ignored her. When Aunt Mavis called my name again, I scooted as fast as I could and entered the yard from the side gate. I cupped some dirt in my hand and rubbed it onto my dress, and decided to tell Aunt Mavis that I fell down running to answer her. I was pouting to booster the effect.

"I thought I heard you call me, Aunt Mavis. I'm sorry, I fell down running to answer you. I hope I didn't tear my dress."

"If you would answer me *before* you tried to be here in front of me, maybe you wouldn't fall down so much."

I guessed that Aunt Mavis was angry, but I wasn't going to test her, not yet.

"All right, Aunt Mavis, I'll try to remember to do that. Should I go bathe and change my clothes?"

"Yes. Don't be too long. We'll go visit your Mom and Dad today."

I shot out of the room as fast as I imagine a bullet flies. I was back in twenty minutes. I was some anxious. I had such happy secret thoughts, "Me and cousin Delia can play jackrocks. We'll maybe even have a fuss today. I'd like a fuss with Delia, whew, I'm kinda some happy." I remembered I needed to carry my own ball for the jackrocks.

That was such a lovely visit to home. I played and talked with my sisters and brothers. I got to go to Delia's house which was just around the corner, and yep, we played jackrocks. But, we didn't have no fuss. We were too glad to see each other.

I liked going to school but not so much for studying books as for the opportunity to play games with other children, and sometimes even with our teachers. It took me a while to realize that after I *was* asked into a game, if I did better than the others, they didn't want me in that game any more. I got to play jump-rope, tag, and hopscotch, but volleyball was the most fun. No one played the Stickball game at school.

Suddenly, I rocked forward hard enough to stand up. Hunger pangs had snapped my mind forward and into the present. I entered the house and went into the kitchen. I stood looking out the kitchen window, but wasn't really seeing anything so I turned my gaze to the inside of the room. "My goodness, how could I let my floor get so dirty? I'll just have to mop this filthy floor right now." I hummed my favorite tune while I attended to those chores. Humming or singing always helped make any work go easy. I felt relieved. Strange, but I didn't feel that the dirt was what I was relieved of. Anyway, I pulled open the drawer beside the sink and took out those two old raggedy pot holders and threw them in the trash. "Now that my kitchen is all cleaned up, I can go sit on the porch and rock until my 'company' arrives."

I started for the front door but got the tightest tug in my belly. "Well, what do you know, I think I'm hungry. I'll just have some cottage cheese with peaches. That oughta taste good." I must have forgotten about being hungry the first time I went into the kitchen because I got busy instead.

I went back onto the front porch and sat in my rocker, but after I had eaten my lunch. It wasn't long before my thoughts had me back in Cayuga.

"Leanna, come here this instant!"

I never could remember whether I touched home plate and scored a point for my team. I do remember that I made a bee-line for the side gate. But, Aunt Mavis had already seen me in the street.

"You, young lady, have no business convoking with those dirty little ragamuffins. They look as if they haven't seen soap and water in a very long time. Do they look the same at school? Oh, God forbid, you don't see them at school, too?" Aunt Mavis frequently used big words like convoking, and I guess that is what made me think she was a very smart woman.

"Yes, Ma'am, they go to school. No, Ma'am, they aren't in my grade. No'm. All the time they wear clean clothes to school." I tried being sassy by sucking in air through my front teeth. Aunt Mavis caught the sarcasm in my reply when she witnessed me jerk my head high and roll my eyes.

"Don't you get sassy-mouth with me, young lady. Just you hear this. I had better not see you ever out there with those ragamuffins again. You don't want to know what I will do. Nice young ladies are never seen unkempt. You come in here and find a game to play with. Or, read a book. I have quite a few children's books."

I sure didn't know Aunt Mavis could get so angry, and I'd been living there for some time now. I thought Aunt Mavis was ready to give me a whipping. But I didn't test her again! When she said I had to do something, I just did it. One of the things she insisted I do every day was take a midday nap. I was already seven years old! I went to elementary school! But like I said, I wasn't gonna test Aunt Mavis again. So, about noon each day of the summer when she called, "Come, Leanna, it's time for you to rest up," I was obedient though I didn't have a clue as to what I was resting up from. Believe it or not, I easily fell asleep, and even felt refreshed when I awoke from my naps.

Truly, my time living with my aunt and uncle was mostly quite enjoyable. But when I look back, I don't know yet why I got to have such freedom choosing the clothes I could buy and wear, and early on even why I could have all those sweet goodies to eat. Unless, that was their subtle way of quickly weaning me from the rest of my family.

I eventually understood the true motive behind the attention Aunt Mavis lavished on me. There were times when Aunt Mavis taught me how to dress my own hair, like combing, braiding, curling, or twisting it into works of art. There were times when Aunt Mavis held brunches with her own friends and included me as one of the invited. The "airs" the guests displayed at the table were my introduction to table etiquette. It didn't take me long to master the art of extending the pinkie finger of the hand that lifted the tea cup. I busied myself watching then imitating the ladies placing their napkins in their laps usually after crossing their legs at the knees. I had great fun pretending to be as grownup as Aunt Mavis's friends.

When they wished to have a "grownups only" discussion, Aunt Mavis would send me in search of something that she knew could not be found—perhaps a keepsake—in a specific place from where it had already been removed. You won't believe that I was all of ten and one half years before I caught on. No, I never eavesdropped. That would have been dishonest and against what I had learned from my parents.

I did lots of wondering while trying to discover the something vital I felt was missing from that scenario. I looked for the reason I was the chosen one, instead of one of some chosen to live with Uncle Norris and Aunt Mavis. To me, it appeared they surely had the means to care for more than one child at the same time.

My system of values was different from those of the rest of my family. My behavior, my dress, all but my inborn virtue, now mimicked the persuasions of Aunt Mavis and Uncle Norris. I knew how to and would glide my bottom into a chair to sit; I'd lay my table napkin across my lap and never rested my elbows on the table during meals; I'd speak now in a soft and demure voice. It pleased me that in propelling myself forward I would place one forward-pointed foot in front of the other, gently and rhythmically, and glide from point A to point B.

I was eleven years old now and the era of my disciplined obedience had begun.

My children need to understand that with the death of Darden, I have come into my "own" time. Darden's death has evaporated the narrow latitude and short longitude of our longtime duet. My children must give me my own space.

Maybe telling the children, "Back off," could be a little harsh, so I'll use a little tact on them. I'll suggest that I'll be doing some hanging out with a few of my peers for a change. They all ought to recognize the 'peer' word, they used it on me when they wanted something they knew was not going to be allowed.

It's all of two years since Darden died, and they still come. Regularly. They're like vultures picking at prey. They do way more than just come here to help me physically, instead they offer unlimited and unsolicited suggestions. They tell me how I should do this, and how I should do that. They even tell me how I should think and what I should think on different ideas. My own children are most annoying now, and I've caught myself screaming at them. "Back off! Leave me alone."

As far back as a few months—after I had screamed my objections to their interferences and fell short of using profanity, or so they thought—I overheard some of their remarks to each other, including, "Mom is showing signs of Alzheimer's." They voiced, to each other, that I seemed quite forgetful lately, like when I put the dish detergent in the refrigerator by mistake, or like when I left the ice cream atop the kitchen counter and it melted as a result.

I swear I believe they are coming over here more frequently. "So what if I left the ice cream out a time or two, or maybe even put the pot holder or dishrag in the fridge instead of the cooked meat?" I still don't accept their abundance of concern for me. Their concern is interfering more and more with the things I want to do. I want to be able to walk a few houses down the street and visit with Chamia, or talk on the telephone late at night with Gracie, or even one of my male friends. Or maybe take a bus ride downtown alone without their frantic concern. They are seriously annoying me with their chaperoning attention.

I've got to close off my space to them, and be with my own group of friends. I must use this time to think for myself, think by myself, and think with myself. Gee, I've got a new motto: think, think, think.

I have found myself focusing too often on my children's uncalled-for-suspicions about my safety, to the point that I'm sorely frustrated. When I'm frustrated, yep, you guessed it, I go onto the front porch and sit in my blue rocking chair and rock until I'm catapulted back to Cayuga.

It was five years before Jason Mallard was well enough to work full time and bring home a decent salary. Norris and Mavis suggested that Daddy work a full year before they returned me to home. Daddy's money, merged with Mom's earnings, was now enough to have the entire family housed under the same roof again. I was beside myself with gladness at being back home with my sisters and brothers. I was going on thirteen years old.

Back home, I formed the closest relationship with my brother Mitchell. He was delighted that I looked up to him for "guidance." He was my hero. Whenever I was pestered by the male acquaintances in the neighborhood, school, or church, it was Mitchell who rescued me from their annoyances. And Mitchell was two years younger than myself.

Mitchell was a bit impish, and that fascinated me. If Mitchell was told to remain on the home grounds while Mom went to town for family necessities, Mitchell would disobey and get into scrapes. He wandered too far from home. Sure, he won the scrapes, but he couldn't hide his escapades from Mom. She wasn't fooled by his skinned-elbow fibs, or the cuts-on-his-cheeks tales.

When Mom sent Mitchell to the elm tree for a "switching branch," he might bring her one too small to be effective for leg-switching. Or one that was too large to be used. Sure, he was testing Mom's patience, but she would merely redirect him to fetch her the right size.

Once, *and only once*, I dared to follow Mitchell on one of his jaunts in Mom's absence from the house. But, oh boy, when I got my legs switched for being disobedient, that was my first and last time hanging with Mitchell. He was unable to convince me again to follow him at doing anything daring.

I had it in my mind since I was back home, that Zeena and I would become bosom buddies, like I had heard sisters did. Sisters should share ideas on what to wear to school, on what to say to fresh-mouthed boys, on whether I could or should wear make-up. I didn't have to depend on Zeena to read stories to me, of course I could do that for myself now. I was a bit disappointed when I realized that Zeena, as a working girl, had very little time to spend with me. It meant sharing little more than a good morning and a good night between us.

Also, because my visits to home had been few and far between, I had lost the friendships of the girls in the neighborhood. They had all focused their attentions elsewhere. I felt quite alone for a long time, even with my own family.

Both of my older brothers, Charles and Jarrett, continued working after Dad returned to work. They were excited over the fact that their employer was sending them to work in New York, and giving them pay raises. Both were well established in relationships with ladies they had met on their jobs and were talking with Dad about getting married. Both got permission from the fathers of the young ladies to marry, which they did, just before they were sent to New York. They had a compassionate employer who also sent along their new wives to work, for as long as the wives wanted to work.

That took Charles and Jarrett out of my life so I had only Zeena with whom I hoped to still become a bosom buddy. I think Zeena felt my pain of isolation because she began to make time to spend with me. We did share some girl secrets, she did express approval or disapproval of my choice of clothes for various occasions. She advised me on whether, when, and how much lipstick I needed. I was thrilled.

In about a year, Zeena was hoping her male friend would ask Daddy for her hand in marriage. He did, they married, and again I suffered the loss of the closeness of a family member. Oh, Mitchell and I were still pals, but I just wouldn't let him convince me to do as he did and said do. Inspite of this one closeness, I imagined that I, in whatever way, was the reason my siblings *wanted* to get away from me. My father took the time and patience to thoroughly explain grownups' thoughts, feelings, attitudes, and behaviors. I finally understood.

As soon as Zeena was no longer working, she started inviting me over to her home mainly for girl talk. I loved her home. Her husband, John Creighton, an entrepreneur, already had purchased the large two-story, five-bedroom, brownstone house on Needle Street. Zeena really impressed me with her talk about how happy John made her, that he lavished her with beautiful gifts weekly. Zeena was most influenced by the fact that John's family overwhelmingly accepted her. Zeena and I, at last, were bosom buddies.

I heavily relied on Zeena's friendship now for the comfort it gave me, especially when my female schoolmates snubbed me. They were all reacting to the unpredictable phases of puberty, and to what I overheard them say was the stark reality of my beauty. "Me, beautiful? Get out of here!" None of these girls hated me, they just didn't want to look into their mirrors and see less than equal beauty in themselves. More and more, I felt like a total stranger among the people I had known years earlier.

Often the male schoolmates thought the antics the girls subjected me to were funny. They, too, were reacting to their own pubescences. Mitchell was my knight in shining armor. He wasn't so understanding of the pranks they played on me. Mitchell had not yet reached the plunging edge of puberty.

At home, I got very busy learning the arts of cooking and sewing from our mother. Sewing came easy to me so I quickly got into more difficult projects than just sewing table scarfs and pillow cases. I got into dressmaking. By the time I was sixteen, I was putting my sewing skill to test by designing my own dresses. Many times when I got too anxious and pinned together the dress parts rather than hand baste, Mom corrected my efforts with words of caution, "Haste makes waste, everytime." I learned the correct way.

I donned my satin rose-colored gown and grey chenille robe after my warm bubble bath, and sat in the soft gold rocker/recliner in the living room. Within minutes, thoughts of my teen years rushed into my head.

"Leanna, get in here girl," shouted Mitchell from the spare bedroom that had been converted into a family room.

"What'cha want, Mitchell? I'm trying to read this magazine."

"Just get in here and find out."

I threw the magazine down on the floor in a huff, pushed myself forward out of the chair, and stomped impatiently into the family room. Mitchell was listening to a phonograph record. He was aware guys were noticing me, and he wanted to get me ready to take over any dance floor.

"I'm here, so what'cha want?"

"Come through the door. You scared of me or what?"

I huffingly stomped all the way into the room, "Naw, should I be? What do you want, Mitch?"

He grabbed me about the waist, placed his left hand in my right hand and suddenly whirled me around in a circle.

"Are you crazy? You coulda let me fall. What are you trying to do?"

"I just thought I'd teach you how to dance. You're fifteen, and gonna need to know how, soon."

"Really, why?" I guessed why, but I wanted him to tell me. I had no idea when or where Mitchell had learned to dance. Anyway, teaching me to dance was a difficult task according to Mitchell who said I moved like I was attached to two left feet. Eventually I did learn the two-step.

The Browns, next door, conducted a music clinic and gave private lessons in piano, clarinet, flute, oboe, and saxophone. Once a year they sponsored a dance for their students who were privileged to bring one guest. We, Mitchell and I, were not students of the Browns but we always got invited.

I was flashing a broad smile and making that gold chair rock faster and faster. That year I wore the green cotton dress I had designed and sewn for myself, and it happened. I turned to acknowledge the soft tap on my left shoulder and looked squarely into the face of a handsome young man. My brow wrinkled, favorably, at his looks as I tried to recall if I had seen him over at the Brown home.

I didn't remember having seen him anywhere before.

Near panic overcame my composure as frantic thoughts besieged me. "Oh, God, is he going to ask me to dance? Do I know how to dance to that music? Do I know any dance steps? Oh, God, what'll I do, what'll I do?" I was also praying that my fright was not showing in my face.

Darden had noticed me standing alone in the doorway to the dance floor. After we had become well acquainted, he told me he thought he had seen my shoulders sag at the start up of a tune, and imagined the cause was that I was the only girl not dancing. He told me that when I turned to acknowledge his tap on my shoulder, he gulped air *hard*, twice, or thrice, before he could speak. He saw me as stunningly beautiful.

This was his overall assessment of my looks, "Your olive-colored skin is as smooth as a plump baby's bottom. Your eyes are large, dark brown pits that are softened only by the white surrounding the pupils. And while your lips bear only a hint of rose, not even that amount of cosmetics is needed to enhance your beauty."

I could see he was wrestling with something internally, but had no idea he was staving off stuttering when he managed, "Please, may I have this dance?"

"I don't really know how to do the Lindy." I hoped I wasn't showing any hint of a struggle to steady my leg wobbles.

"And I'm not the best at it either. Then, maybe you will dance with me when the next slow record is played."

"Well, all right. But I don't really know how to dance any kind of dance." Now I was panicking; I thought I had said the wrong thing and my words would push him away. I resolved to try, though, for I did want to try to fit in. Meeting him and having this short conversation had made me quite thirsty. I said I would return after I got myself a glass of punch.

"Stay, I'll get us each a glass," he offered.

More frantic moments as I longed to have Mitchell by my side retelling me what to do. He had told me something that I was never to forget. Fine time for me *not* to remember. I squeezed together my buttocks, a trick I had learned while living with Aunt Mavis and Uncle Norris, which had the effect of stilling the thought processes, thus calming me. I inhaled deeply then expelled the air slowly. "Aah, it works. I remember. Mitchell said I was to 'think on the beat and rhythm of the music and your body's movements will conform.' That's exactly what he said! Now, I'll see if it works."

The next record playing had a beat suitable for the two-step dance, and Darden and I entered the dance floor.

Temporarily our conversation lacked gusto. We talked about the weather and how mild the spring was so early in the season before either one of us revealed our name.

"I don't believe I told you my name. I'm Darden. Darden Swelton. And what might your name be?"

"My name is Leanna."

"Are you one of Mrs. Brown's music students?"

"No, I just live next door. Our families have long been good friends, so Mrs. Brown always invites us to the occasions of honoring her students."

"Say, take a look at that fellow over there, the one in the brown suit. He is one smooth dancer."

"Oh, that's just my brother Mitchell. I guess maybe he can dance."

"Well, how about that. I've known Mitchell for some time. Mitchell plays in the same musical band as my best friend Samuel. Samuel is a second year piano student with Mrs. Brown. I'm his guest. Sam is right over there by the lamp table."

"I've often seen your friend either arriving or leaving Mrs. Brown's home."

"So, you are Mitchell's sister." An opportunity had opened for Darden to ask, "Do you think that I might call upon you sometimes?"

I know I must have looked stupid, but I couldn't help flashing at least twenty pearlies at him. Inside, my belly was a flash of fire, at least that's what it felt like, all because I liked him being interested in me.

"I am only seventeen. You will have to get my father's permission to be my gentleman caller."

"I'm nineteen. You don't suppose that your father will think me too old to call upon you, do you?"

"I don't know." The conversation switched topics. I felt some pain of anxiety at that moment, and I began wishing, with all my heart, that Darden would not be scared away. I wished he would go forth and ask my father if he could come calling. I was at that moment aware of those kinds of feelings that my father had fully explained to me is usually what happens to near-young adults.

Well, Darden did talk to my daddy within the week, and he won Daddy's approval, and he did begin a courtship with me. But, oh my goodness, whenever we passed someone on the street, the after-flow of their voices usually sounded like they were voiceing their approval of our relationship. No, it did not matter to me what they thought. I had my father's approval.

I am just now realizing that I'm spending an awful lot of time sitting in this rocker/recliner, and that I'm really entertaining myself with my memories.

To a memory flash, I laughed hard and out loud. I remembered the exact words Darden had told me exchanged between him and my father.

"My left leg began to shake. I tried leaning hard on my left foot to stop the shake. Then my leg ached. When I shifted my weight to my right foot, I got a crippling cramp in my left leg. To your father, my reaction to that cramp must have seemed like I was beginning a dance, because he displayed a frown on his face that scared the be-Jesus out of me. I just knew he was going to say 'no' to me.

"I quickly recovered and let him know that I was experiencing a cramp in my leg and was merely trying to shake the muscles loose to release the cramp."

"Certainly glad you informed me, young man, because I was about to tell you to get lost. Anyone who acts weird like you were just doing, certainly does not need to come calling on my daughter."

Darden said my daddy shook his hand, glinted a smile, paused while looking him sternly in the eye, then gave his permission to call upon me.

And thus began the courtship of Darden Swelton and me, Leanna Mallard.

CHAPTER 3

▼

LEANNA AND DARDEN

The wall clock ticked. Loudly. Inside my head I blurted, "All right, so I know the hour." But I remained seated until one hour more ticked away.

"They will come. They will surely come. All of them."

The thoughts in my head were seeking some action.

I pondered over the idea of making a schedule based on their invasions of my privacy. "Hey, just do it. It ought to be fun, having a game to keep up with them. It shouldn't take much to do a schedule. That way I'll know for sure who was here, when they were here, and why they were here. And best of all, I'll know exactly what they did while they were here."

In my sudden excitement, I pulled a tad too hard on the lamp table drawer and out it came, spilling its contents onto the floor. I just slid from the sofa cushion to the floor, and took the opportunity to clean out that drawer.

"It just doesn't make sense to keep stuffing things in here merely to get them out of sight of company. *Company!* My children are more like foreign dignitaries, they think they have the right to do anything they please in my house and get away with it." Certainly, I know I'm talking to myself. "I know I did not put this bottle brush in that drawer. That does it! I'm making that schedule today, right now! I *will* be taking part in the events going on in my home."

I returned the cleaned drawer to the lamp table, and positioned myself back up on the sofa, but before I could draw the first mark on my note pad, I reclined my head against the sofa back.

There it was. I was seeing it now as if for the first time. Maida had had the picture of me, taken when I was eighteen, enlarged. She hung it above my favorite gold chair. A big grin wormed its way onto my face just then. I remembered why I had this picture made for Darden.

Darden continued seeing me long after Daddy gave his permission. One day he told me, "Daytime, nightime, any time, you, Leanna, are the beautiful vision that engulfs my mind. You are like a disease, but a disease that I don't wish to be rid of."

Darden often seized opportunities to say such things that would build any girl's self-esteem, whether or not it was true. And his words certainly boosted my self-esteem, but I don't think to the point that one would say my head was swelled.

Darden, at the outset of our relationship, told me that he had been seeing a couple of young ladies that he now had to explain his change of heart to. There was one young lady that did not want to give him up. To that bit of revelation I informed Darden that I would not entertain having an altercation with any young woman who was interested in him.

"Get your business straight with these young women or you just get lost."

The particular young woman who was obsessed with Darden was named Letitia. He said he had told her once, "Letitia, you're the most striking beauty in town." He said she took that to mean she had unlimited opportunities to encroach upon his time. He needed to become untangled with her, and after some weeks of difficulty, he finally succeeded. It was unfortunate that she pressured him at the annual

Wharf's Teen Public Dance, for it was there in front of all those present, that he loudly protested the attention she was giving him. He said it truly hurt him to cut her loose in that manner, but she brought it upon herself. He had told her several times that he was in love with me, and had included, "My intentions are to marry Leanna as soon as she will accept my proposal. I have her father's approval."

It was about this time that Gertrude and I became best friends. We had met at school. Within a year Gertrude was transferred to a different school—required when her family moved to a new neighborhood—but she and I remained friends. We kept in touch by sending notes through the mail. We would meet at football and softball events that were played on sandlots. We would go together to town to shop. We even swapped tales that *only* a best friend must know. Little did I imagine that very soon I was in for a tremendous letdown when I learned my friend was not what she appeared to be.

Gertrude was dishonest. All this time, Gertrude had focused on, and absorbed, all the information I had told her about my relationship with Darden, and was now trying to use the same in her efforts to take Darden away from me. Darden had cautioned me that he thought Gertrude was coming on to him, and had asked me to say nothing of his suspicions. I did as he suggested, but, when Gertrude stole the friendship ring that Darden had given me, I lashed out to crush her like a boa constrictor crushes its prey.

Neither I nor Gertrude were inclined to physical violence. She insisted, "I found this ring. You never had this ring. Yours might've looked like this, but that's all. This ring I found."

Because I came so close to not being in control of my emotions and my impatient arms, I didn't choose to stay friends with her, and told her so. When I reported the "loss" of my ring to Darden and began dripping several tears, he just wrapped his arms around me and held me close for a long while. We made no occasion to speak of the ring incident again.

Zeena was married for five years when another crisis plagued the Mallard family. Daddy had been laid off his job; his company was suffering great financial losses. Even with monies being sent by my brothers from New York, Daddy was unable to continue payments on our home. It was in December of 1916 when he put our house up for rent. Daddy, Mama, myself, Mitchell, and Odetta had been invited to move in with Zeena and John. We accepted.

My family's move to Zeena's and John's home did not cause any interruption in my relationship with Darden. In fact, Darden came calling every day from that time. Many times, when we did not go to the movie show, we would stroll in the park located beneath the Chidra Viaduct. The Chidra was paved with cobblestones, as were many of the streets in Cayuga. The clopping sounds, made by horses drawing carriages across the Viaduct, were likened to a sonata for a symphonic orchestra. Darden and I often made up names for the varying sounds of the many tempos. Funny how love made our world go round. We were so enamored of each other.

On one of the days that we spent in that park, Darden ventured a "what if" conversation with me. "What if you were in your middle twenties, would you already be married, want to be married, or not speculate on marriage?"

Darden caught me by surprise and I felt so bashful. My eyelids began blinking rapidly, so I lowered my glance before I returned an answer.

"I think I would want to already be married. Ladies who reach their twenty-fifth birthday and are not married are called spinsters. Behind their backs, of course. I hope I won't get called one." I really wasn't hinting that I wanted us to be married to each other, and I didn't notice that that was the way he took it. Darden continued, "What if you were married, would you want to have a family of two, or four, or more children?"

Now I felt I was glowing, and if he didn't change the bent of this exchange, he would see that I was glowing.

"I think I would like to be a mother. And if I had a good husband, I would want to please his wishes on how many children."

I was so nervous that I began to pick at the patch of grass protruding from under the side of the big rock next to where I sat. Darden noticed my nervousness.

He changed the subject by asking, "Would you like to go to the Wharf? I think I'd like something to snack on."

My sudden laughter was almost inaudible.

He asked, "Did I say something funny?"

"No, I remembered a time, years ago, when my older brothers took me to the Wharf. I ate several crabmeat sandwiches and became very ill. At first, everyone thought the meat must not have been fresh, but that was not the problem. I simply didn't know when enough was enough. I spent the night in pain and begged not to be given a nasty tasting medicine to make me all better. I vowed never to eat crabmeat sandwiches again. Silly me. I love crabmeat."

Darden had gleaned enough information about me to know that I was the woman he wanted to marry. He promised himself that at first opportunity he would ask my daddy for my hand in marriage. Darden asked and Daddy gave his approval. And, I just know that I was as anxious as Darden to begin an experience that I thought could be as happy as the one my sister Zeena talked about.

It took me all of two weeks to design and sew my wedding dress. I asked Zeena to stand as my witness. Darden asked his best friend, Samuel, to stand as his witness. So, that Saturday of the third week of July in 1917, Darden and I were married in Aunt Claudine's home. Aunt Claudine was my daddy's oldest sister.

We moved into our own place, but we didn't go away on a honeymoon. The reason was because Darden had received the Selective Service Draft Board's notice which classified him as available for United States military service, and he knew to be ready if and when he got called upon. The United States was engaged in World War I.

We had been married all of three months when he was summoned for active duty with the U.S. Army. He prayed that once his military duty was over and he was returned home, he could resume his job as top baker with the famous Jordeen Bakery.

Mitchell, now old enough to work, had been given permission to tour with a musical band which meant there was one less mouth to feed at the Creighton home. Dad had been working odd jobs for almost a year before he found steady work, and that was only a part-time job. He worked at that job for only one month before influenza courted his body once more. Pneumonia treaded close on the heels of this flu attack. Dad was a very sick man. Mom was of no help to Dad, or anyone. Mom was soon to give birth after a rather difficult pregnancy.

John Creighton, Zeena's husband, was a stalwart and wonderful man in my family's eyesight. We loved him partially because he shared Zeena with her Dad, Mom, siblings, and all of our problems. He was there for us to lean on whenever we needed him. We were in dire need of his strength in just two weeks when the flu and pneumonia dealt Dad a fatal blow.

Though Mom delivered a healthy boy eleven months after we all moved in with Zeena, her pregnancy had irreparably impaired her health. Dad died one week after Mom gave birth, and the occasion of death pushed her into a deep depression.

Mom never told anyone that she was experiencing nearly unbearable pain after the birth. But, we learned later that her pain was the result of a certain procedure that had been performed on her. Following the birth, Mom's medical attendants made her stand on her feet, then they violently shook her forcing the expulsion of the placenta—a procedure that had been used on colored women during slavery. Mom suffered Prolapsus Uteri, a common disease that made her vulnerable to Tetanus Neonatorum, a frequent cause of death. Mom did not respond favorably to medicinal care given her in the two remaining years of her life.

I had been married for six months when Dad died. With Dad's death and Darden's separation from me due to the war, I felt very alone. I hoped Darden would not feel my kind of loneliness, so I had a photo shop take my picture, and I sent it off to him. The same picture my daughter Maida had enlarged. It now hangs in my living room above the gold chair.

Darden's tour of duty began and was spent on foreign soil once his basic training was completed. Although he never reached the front-line, he came close. His unit's specific job was to ready suplies of arms, road equipment, clothing, etc., needed by the men who were on the front lines.

The day after Darden left for his foreign duty, I took a job as take-in girl at the Spider Laundry and Cleaners. I had hopes that by so occupying my time, Darden's time away would seem shorter. It wasn't long before I knew I was expecting our first child. But I wasn't ready to tell Darden about my pregnancy or my job.

It turned out that Darden was gone only seven months before being wounded by a stray bullet. He was delivering some equipment to the front-line soldiers. The front-line soldiers had to retreat just as he arrived on the scene. He backed his vehicle to turn it around. At that moment a spray of bullets came through the brush. Darden was struck in the left shoulder. Strangely enough, he had not felt the penetration. He became aware of a rush of blood down his left side. He made it back to his unit's headquarters, then promptly passed out. Not from pain. Fright!

Darden was told he would wear a souvenir for life. The bullet could not be removed safely. His intense concentration on getting well helped him to heal in little more than two weeks. His service tour was over. He was sent home and honorably discharged in two weeks more.

I was deeply puzzled as to which of my news events I should tell Darden first—my father's death, my mother's illness, my job acquisition, or my pregnancy. I blabbed my pregnancy first. As he held me dearly, in his warm bear hug while sopping wet kisses all over my face,

I managed to tell him that Dad had died, and that Mom was very ill. I no longer thought the news of me getting my very first job was of any importance.

In just under two months later, I delivered a baby boy. Unfortunately, this child expired just seconds after passing through the birth channel. He was not quite full term with lungs that had developed at a much slower rate than was normal. The hospital had insufficient equipment to cope with his problems.

Darden, after witnessing the effects the negative events of the past year had on me, vowed to himself that he would protect me, his "delicate little flower" from further harm. He began by forbidding me to work outside the home. Mr. Dancer, President and CEO of Jordeen Bakery, did give Darden his old job back with a substantial increase in pay.

No one, especially Darden nor I, envisioned we would have a long future together. One day, Rastivus, a friend to our son Braxton, asked, "Mr. Swelton, how'd you do it? How'd you do fifty years together?"

Darden shifted his position in his chair, looked the young fellow in the eye, smiled a slow smile, then declared, "It wasn't easy." The combination of Darden's smile and his words played havoc with the young man's funny bone. The young man laughed hard enough to have to excuse himself to the bathroom. Rastivus, himself now old, still smiles broadly when he looks upon my face and into my eyes.

During the first twenty-four years of our sixty-seven years together, Darden and I became the parents of Shannon, Darrell, Edril, Larson, Maida, Braxton, Cordice, Racina, and Neva.

My first "activity schedule" was all of one month old before I chose to examine what was happening. I had used ruled notebook paper to make the schedule that began with the month of February. I evenly marked off fourteen vertical columns on each side, then in sequence at the top, numbered them one through twenty-eight. I wrote down the child's name in the two-inch wide column at the left side of the page, and the initials of any activity the child performed, that is, a "v" for vacuum, "hc" for hall closet, "co" for cook, et cetera, in the vertical column whose number represented the date of the month.

To my surprise, Edril's daughter Suilela had visited twenty of the days of February. Everytime she came, she busied herself vacuuming and dusting for "my favorite grandmother." She dabbed my silk roses with rose oil once a week which left my house smelling lovely.

So, twenty-eight days after beginning the schedule of my children's visits and noting the activities performed, I was seeing a pattern.

Cordice lived some two hundred miles away and was a non-working wife who visited ten days of the twenty-eight days. She stayed five days each visit. While here, she busied herself in my hall closet attempting to bring some order to the clutter of bathtowels, washcloths, bathmats, and bars of soap in one area, and dishtowels, dishcloths, and cleaning detergents in another.

We always had this exchange of words. "Mother, how is it that one person can create such a mess in this little tiny space? How can you know what is in here with everything unfolded and mixed together?"

"Actually, with you in there now, that makes for more than one person, doesn't it?" Meanwhile, I mused over how bored one can get with the obvious.

"I'm only in here to clean up this mess, behind you."

"So, that's why you're in my closet! I didn't send you in there for anything, Cordice." I hesitated. "Or, did I?"

"Oh, Mother. Sometimes you're impossible."

"Impossible? How do you mean that?"

Cordice would venture no further conversation or comments. She'd roll her eyes, shake out and refold each piece that she picked up, then place the folded piece in its special place. And so, with such an exchange I succeeded in cutting off one avenue of discomfort for myself.

Racina equaled Suilela's twenty days of visiting, yet their paths crossed only once in that time span. Suilela came during the weekday mornings, and Racina came late weekday afternoons and into early evenings. I studied my schedule and had another realization. Racina was on the receiving end of the "do for's" intended for me. You see, Racina came by to eat, converse a little, sleep, and then go home. This behavior I had not minded back then. It is now two years after Darden's death, and I do mind.

Larson lives right here in town, as does Racina and Neva, but he claims to be so occupied with his social club activities after his regular working hours that he might visit only two times of any week. His visits produce mostly conversation, which I usually appreciate, all but the part that includes the questions that I consider are grilling me about my daily activities.

"Larson, you ask me the same questions each time you stop by. Why is that? I tell you that I'm just fine every time you ask. And I am, just fine."

"I think I'm showing great concern for your well-being when I ask how you are, Mama. If I didn't ask about your health, how would you feel?"

"I think I would feel fine. Trust me, if I feel anyways not in the ordinary, I'll let you or Racina or Neva know about it."

"Well, you can just get used to it, because it's more than just a courtesy act to inquire about my Mother's health. Did you have any solicitors call on you today?"

"Solicitors? You mean someone trying to sell me something?"

"Yes."

"Some man from THE Roofing Company called yesterday about my roof. He said he was passing by the other day and noticed how old my roof looked, so he's coming by tomorrow at four o'clock for me to sign the papers to have the work done before I have some serious problems."

"You see, Mama, when I ask how you are, or what's happening, this is what I'm getting at. There're always these scam artists out there preying on older people, on widows especially, who take from them everything they own. And how do they know who is a widow and who isn't? They get that information mainly from reading the newspaper obituaries. Promise me, Mama, you won't ever sign any paper for any reason unless me or Racina or Neva is here. Okay?"

"And I thought you knew me better than that, honey. I learned well from your father. Yes, I promise, I won't sign any paper, no matter how urgent the solicitor sounds. When I tell them to come back at such and such a time, and they claim they'll be gone elsewhere by that time, that's when I tell them they need to go elsewhere now, not later. Sure, I've made a few get angry because I wouldn't sign some paper or say yes to whatever. I'd just slam the door shut, and lock it."

"That's another thing, Mama, never unlock your storm door to anyone. If they want you to read something, tell them to mail it to you, then just close the big door and lock it. That way they don't get the chance to sucker you with a few sugary words. Okay?"

"Okay, honey. I hear you loud and clear." I stroked his left cheek and smiled at his sincere concern.

As for Neva, she was always in a hurry to get her visits over with. Oh, she had nothing against me. She had to get home to her three youngsters aged seven, eight, and ten. Her children were not bad, they just had very high IQs and seemed to take great pleasure in one-upmanship with each other's intellect no matter the category. This usually meant utter chaos in that one household. When Neva was not on time getting home to them, the screams they directed at each other could be heard a few houses away. Visits from Neva were strictly to offer me transportation to anywhere away from home and back.

"Mother, do you need to get anything from the store?"

Or, "Mother, when did you tell me you had to go to the beauty parlor?"

"Oh, that's Wednesday, honey. But, Pectola is going to get her hair done at the same time. She will be stopping by for me. Thanks, anyway. And we did our grocery shopping yesterday morning so I don't need anything right now."

"All right. Mom, I've gotta go, the children will be home fifteen minutes earlier today and I need to be there with them."

I wondered why Neva would choose a day that left her little time to share herself. "See you next time, honey." I waved goodbye from my doorway.

And Neva would be off to her own place.

My schedule "game" had produced good results—I now knew who came by, when they came by, and what they were up to while they were here. My first month's schedule revealed that their concern for me was sheer love. But sometimes, their overprotection made me cantankerous. To keep some semblance of peace, I knew that I had to be the one to concede to my children. I decided to allow their concerns into my life, peaceably, for as long as they realized when they were entering into my "space" and needed to back off.

So, by checking my schedule once a month, I learned that each child, grandchild, and great-grandchild intensified his or her loving concern for me. And for now, that meant I needed only to utter an occasional, "Back off."

CHAPTER 4

▼

DARDEN'S BACKGROUND

Darden had not known his father, but he did know something about him. Lionel Swelton had died of pneumonia two months after Darden's birth. His mother Beah would care single handedly for four young children under the age of twelve—himself, a sister two years older than he, another sister but five years older than himself, and a brother who had turned eleven only six months earlier. At the first sign of their father's illness, Darden's four siblings older than twelve years found employment and helped with the family's finances. Their father had been a Methodist minister. His Christian followers lent helping hands whenever it became necessary. Someone from church usually accommodated Mrs. Swelton with any heavy chores. Although Lionel's death dealt a terrible blow to the family, they were able to get along without too many difficulties.

Darden's parents had met when each secured work in the same household. His father was the butler and his mother was the maid. These jobs were not live-in positions. Each returned to his own home at the end of their ten-hour work day. It took a long time before they were able to get acquainted. In their positions at *The Mansion*, they were not allowed to converse with each other. They must only follow the daily verbal instructions of the owners-managers of *The Mansion*. Three times a day the master or the mistress of *The Mansion*—a home for six to eight displaced teen girls—would appear and give them their work instructions.

They finally had the chance to converse one day when Beah tripped over her skirttail, fell, and struck her head lightly on the edge of the kitchen countertop. Lionel Swelton had heard the commotion and came to investigate. He found Beah Singer, sprawled and dazed on the kitchen floor.

He thought, "Certainly there can be no objection to my inquiring if she is badly hurt." So, he went to her rescue. He helped her to her feet and asked her, "Are you hurt badly, Miss? May I be of some assistance?"

"I feel a bit light in the head. Would you help me over to that chair? Maybe I have time to rest. I need a second or so to pull myself together. Then I'll start the evening meal."

At that precise moment the mistress of the house appeared and heard them talking to each other. She dismissed them both from employment right there on the spot. *The Mansion* mistress refused to hear about what had just happened.

It behooved Lionel that he alone was at fault for them losing their jobs. Inasmuch as they were no longer employed they were free to talk with each other however they chose. When they left the great house, Lionel was in no hurry to leave Beah to some unknown fate. She could be seriously hurt as a result of that unfortunate fall. It was a legitimate excuse to walk her home.

There he met her mother and father. He immediately asked permission to call upon Beah from time to time. Lionel had thought himself in love with Beah from the day they were employed, but he knew he would need to go very slow in building a solid relationship. He feared this beautiful, slim, statuesque, chocolate-colored woman would reject him. Permission was granted.

His calling day was Sunday. He would come early enough to walk with Beah and her family to their place of worship. Beah was permitted to sit toward the rear of the church with Lionel and some other young people. The budding friendship between Lionel and Beah blossomed quickly. Their life-long compatibility was shored up when they chose to become friends before starting a courtship.

Neither Lionel nor Beah experienced difficulty in finding new jobs after being dismissed from *The Mansion.* Again, they were working together as butler and maid, but in a totally different environment. Each secretly wished they would one day be married to each other.

Lionel was known as a frugal young worker. He had learned about thrift first from his mother. She had been widowed before her last child, Lionel, was grown. He had saved quite a sum of money. He'd have some security to offer his chosen young maiden when he felt he was ready to marry. Beah was his chosen young maiden. Soon he proposed marriage to her and she accepted. They were married, and shortly afterwards began a family of their own.

Lionel's mother was a pious woman. She had taught each of her children specific Bible passages she hoped they would not forget. She was rather persuasive, insisting that each child, "Walk the walk of the talk they talked." She tried to persuade her children that the right course in life was to be kind to people, to be of some constructive help to people. Her persuasiveness prevailed with Lionel, who, now a married young man, saw fit to pursue deeper meanings of the many books of the Bible. And so, he studied to become a minister. In all of eleven years, he completed the required studies. Lionel was ordained a minister in the Methodist Church, a move that greatly pleased his wife Beah.

Lionel had been a minister for about ten years when he was called to the home of one of his parishioners believed near death. Back then, being called to one's home meant passing the word along by mouth until it reached the intended person's ears. That very cold and wet January night, Lionel readied himself for the journey some two miles away. Walking became slippery as the dirt road iced over. Icy, gale force winds, enveloped Lionel's body in a tight hug under his coattail. But his ministerial duty was to administer to all of his parishioners whenever he was needed. And he was needed.

That trip was the beginning of Lionel Swelton's own fight for survival. In spite of such weather brutality, he forged ahead.

Mr. Grayson, the parishioner, was barely alive when the Reverend Swelton arrived. Final rights were given Mr. Grayson, and the Reverend Swelton prayed with his family. Because the weather had turned so bitter in the three hours it took Lionel to make the journey, Mrs. Grayson invited their pastor to stay the night and recover from the onslaught of the weather. The rainwear he wore had been of little consequence in that kind of weather. He was soaked clear to the skin.

The next morning arrived and Lionel, in clothes that had not thoroughly dried overnight, headed out for his home to prepare for the funeralizing of Mr. Grayson. The long walk home in the still chilling and blustery winds took its toll on Lionel. He would one month later succumb to pneumonia. He had not had sufficient time to coddle and cuddle his newborn son, Darden.

CHAPTER 5

▼

REFLECTIONS OF THE EARLY YEARS

Frequently, like practically every other day, I open this glass cabinet and take out one of my photo albums. Looking in these albums helps me remember what each of my children was like as each grew up. In fact, unless one has something concrete to refer to, relying only on one's memory to sequence the events of each child's primer years presents a huge difficulty. That is why everyone should have some sort of permanent record of the events in their lives. If one does not keep photos, then keeping a journal or diary for each child could be the next best thing.

Because Darden was long regarded as the paternal glue of this family, I, and proudly so, padded my ego with, "And I am the maternal glue." Darden had a grandiloquent philosophy of life and I praised him highly because of it. I believe much of his philosophy invaded the minds of our children which procreated cohesive personalities in them. We were immensely pleased about it.

We had two live births within three years after the stillbirth loss of our first child. Shannon was our first eventful birth. She was indeed the apple of Darden's eye. His last gesture before departing for work every morning was to place a lip-kiss or a finger-carried kiss on her sleeping forehead. She would still be in slumberland at five o'clock in the morning. And when he arrived home from work, he'd sweep her up off the floor and whirl her around in the air. Shannon was giddy with joy and fright. She sure loved her daddy.

Darrell (we didn't want a boy named junior) was born a year and a half later. We hoped he would be a replica of Darden, especially in looks and attitude. We'd hear people say about Darrell, "He's the spitting image of his daddy." Or, "Well, will you look at that resemblance!" And, "He sure didn't take anything after his mother."

In less than five years of marriage, Darden and I began experiencing financial problems, same as the rest of the country was suffering. The stock market began to flutter. Back and forth. Up, then down. Enough to give a great deal of the nation's population butterflies in their stomachs. All were wondering what the stock market fluctuations were forecasting. Darden sensed he should look for a second job, just in case all the stock market activity meant something sinister. He wanted to get that "bird in the hand" now.

Darden was one lucky person. He found a second job. Work hours were such that he would be able to see his children wide awake before he must leave home for one job. His reporting time for his old job was moved up to 7 A.M. He would arrive home from that job by 4 P.M., have dinner, play for an hour with the children, then set off for his second job. This job used up four more hours before he would be home again. Ideal timing for moments alone with me. Our children would be sound asleep for the night.

On a day that I chose to take Shannon and Darrell to the public park, Darrell fell ill to the worst of the children's communicable diseases—measles. I did everything my doctor advised me to do for Darrell. Even so, Darrell had to be hospitalized because I was unable to control the fevers he suffered daily.

State and county health departments, extending regulations of eighteenth century maritime quarantine laws into all of their counties, placed quarantine notices on the homes of suspect individuals in their efforts to stop the spreading of the zymotic diseases—measles, consumption, diptheria, whooping cough, croup. The increases in these communicable diseases were the direct result of the rather rapid growth of towns—due to an influx of peoples as well as products and goods needed to build roads, houses, railroads, provide food, and the like.

Even after one-quarter of the twentieth century had passed, still the County Health Department tacked 12-inch square "Quarantined" posters on the outer front and back walls of a family's living quarters. This meant that no visitors were to be allowed on the premises during the entire time those posters remained visible. Most people thought this a rather dumb idea, because the financial provider for the family could go to and return from his place of employment in spite of the warning posters.

Practically all of the employees had small children. The employees all handled each others product parts. They had been told that the diseases were being spread by handling the materials that any diseased carrier had handled. Nobody, but nobody, knew for sure who a diseased carrier was.

I thought it strange that Shannon had not fallen victim to this disease, but she remained quite healthy. It happened some ten days after Darrell was hospitalized. I was rocking in my rocker on the front porch, watching Shannon as she played in the dirt pile in the yard. I shuddered from the chill that suddenly came over me. I brought my rocking chair to a halt and perched on the edge of the chair. A foreboding feeling was flooding my entire body, and I felt a tear rolling down my left cheek. I called out to Shannon, then rose from my chair to meet Shannon halfway the stairs leading to the porch, and I picked her up in my arms and clutched her tightly. It was but a moment later before I would know what that strange feeling was all about.

My eyes caught sight of the red and white ambulance driving slowly down our street, slowing even more as it got closer to our home. It stopped in front of our door. I couldn't help letting out an agonizing scream.

I knew!

Two male workers manned the ambulance. I asked that they go fetch my husband from his job and escort him home. My knees weakened now, as I freed Shannon from my clutches. She glided down the front of my body to the porch floor. My eyes closed nudging me into oblivion. One of the ambulance attendants prevented me suffering any physical harm as he managed to support my collapse. He then propped me upright in my rocking chair. He waited there by my side and kept watch over Shannon until his co-worker returned to the home with Darden.

The news was that Darrell had contracted, in addition to the measles, another devastating communicable disease—whooping cough. This combination of diseases literally usurped the breath right out of our child. Darrell did not reach his third birthday.

In the days following Darrell's death, I wouldn't allow myself to dwell on what could have or would have or should have been. Instead, I furiously availed myself for my housework, for my daughter, and for Darden. And something else—for my church.

I admit that sometimes I felt that God had abandoned me. Yet I couldn't think of anything that I was doing wrong to anyone or anything. "Why me, God, why this punishment?" I wondered that often and secretly. I began participating in activities at my church. I guess I was exhibiting great faith to be appointed as one of the junior stewardesses in my church. And trust me, I was having no difficulty with juggling my wife and mother responsibilities with my assigned church activity.

My first church activity was as a soprano singer in the church choir. The church members, choir members, and church musician all claimed I had such a beautiful voice. I became so enthralled with my church choir activity that I regretted having all those negative thoughts about God punishing me for any wrong doing.

Within the next two years our family experienced joy and more tragedy at about the same time. The joy—that I was with child; the tragedy—that back in Darden's hometown, his twice-widowed mother had been stricken with a life-threatening respiratory illness.

Darden was the only son that anyone in his family knew the where-abouts of, so he was summoned to his mother's home to assist her. He felt that I was too far along in my pregnancy to risk traveling some two hundred miles to be at his side. So, Shannon and I stayed behind in Cayuga longingly awaiting Darden's early return.

His early return was not to be. Darden's mother, Mrs. Evernest, suf-fered a setback and succumbed to her illness. Darden remained in Graybar for several months after the funeral to put closure on all of his mother's business ventures. She had not left a will, so the homestead was to be equally shared by him and his siblings, according to state law.

Eventually, it was decided that, since Darden didn't own a home-stead but his siblings did, he should be the one to move his family into their mother's home. Darden agreed only after he had secured gainful employment there in Graybar.

"Hum, I thought I had my blue shawl around me a while ago. Oh, here it is, it just slipped off my shoulders onto the back of the sofa. I must have dozed off by the way I'm slouched here." To better browse through the photo album I leaned over on my right elbow, and memo-ries flooded my mind as though it were just yesterday when I first walked into the beautiful homestead formerly kept by my mother-in-law, Mrs. Evernest.

It was such a beautiful home. There were three bedrooms and a living room all on the upstairs floor. The dining room and the kitchen were all of the downstairs floor. The house had a total of five exits to the outdoors. The upstairs entrance door, front center of the house, opened inside into a vestibule. The door from the vestibule on the right allowed one to enter the living room and pass through into one bedroom. This bedroom had a side exit to the outdoors with steps going down to ground level. The door from the vestibule on the left permitted entrance into a second bedroom through which one could pass into yet a third bedroom.

This room was similar in features to the first bedroom, plus it had steps on the inner wall. These steps led down into the kitchen. To the right of the kitchen was the entrance into the dining room. The exterior doors of these two rooms opened onto a porch. On the left side of the porch was an enclosed toilet. A similar shaped room, on the opposite side of this porch, was a pantry that contained shelving for food stocks and all kinds of cooking utensils.

The house held but one clothes closet. It was a huge walk-through. This closet was centered between the living room and the second bedroom, but south and beyond the fireplaces of those two rooms. The closet was so large that I thought it must have been the family's nursery during the childbearing years.

This stately old mansion (that is just what it was to me and the children), sat atop a sloped mound which leveled at the rear of the house. A water well had been the central borderline for this and three other properties. The well was now dry. The families who shared joint ownership of these properties had the well dirt-filled to prevent any accidents. They knew their children would constantly be playing all about the grounds.

No one in my family had any difficulties meeting and becoming fast friends with the neighbors. Perhaps our children, again numbering two with the birth of our son Edril, shortly before relocating with Darden, had plenty to do with our compatible relationships. The children played very well together. A neighbor told me about a Methodist church located close by. Though I had been raised in the Baptist faith, I had no real hangups about any other denominations. I always believed we worshipped the same omniscient God above.

But, because I had never wanted to become involved with a Catholic church, I remarked, "Darden, I simply don't feel comfortable telling my week's events to a middle man, a priest. I prefer to go directly to God in my own way. I know He's up there, listening. And seeing. And understanding."

And Darden had answered, "I wasn't trying to take away your right to choose. I just felt that being close to any worship hall would be a convenience. Especially since we have the children, and may sometimes worship into the evenings."

"I understand your position, Darden, and I appreciate your thoughtfulness. But just know, should we have to live elsewhere, and near a Catholic church, I won't worship at that church, even if we all do worship the same God."

I thought with that exchange of words I had gotten things straight. Little did I know. Darden, at his every opportunity, subtly tried to steer me towards the Methodist places of worship. Darden had been raised in the Methodist faith. At this time in our lives, he should have understood that it was all right. I had no objections to worshipping in the Methodist faith.

I readily got involved in the local Methodist church soon after being told its location. I was eager to get on with pleasing the God I believed was the creator and savior of the universe. My first duty in my new place of worship was that of an usher serving on the first Sunday of each month.

Our family began growing faster than I had anticipated. Our children were all healthy and beautiful, and I gracefully accepted what I was given. Another boy, Larson, and a girl, Maida, had joined our family. Darden was delighted to no end. He adored our children, and showed his love by spending much of his free time coddling and cuddling our offspring. Still, he remained the sole financial provider of our family.

Other than on Sundays and the first hours of my Saturdays, I was very busy keeping the family in clothes. I guess had I not believed in keeping the Sabbath, I probably would have washed that day too. The clothes I hung on the wire clothesline which stretched twice across the width of the back yard, were snow-white clean and the brightest of color. It pleased me immensely to be able to get the children-worn clothes so clean. I did it by putting them in water in a huge black cauldron that I hung over an open fire in our back yard. I then added my own homemade lye soap and let the pot boil. If it rained, I put the clothes in water in a tin tub atop my wood stove in the kitchen. My clothes got equally as clean.

When our children were small, I began giving each some small chore to tend to on a daily basis. I made weekly charts showing what each should do. That way I was certain that it would be a few weeks before any child repeated a task. The boys washed dishes as did the girls. The girls hung out the daily wash as did the boys. In fact, the only chore not shared by boys and girls was the woodchopping. That was boys task only, and not before each had reached his thirteenth birthday.

Our children were most obedient of which we were very proud. We would have no reason to complain about them.

My next door neighbor, north, told me one day, "Mrs. Swelton, I can bank on finding you rocking in your blue chair on your front porch just as certain as the day is fair and warm. I hear you plenty times laughing and I guess you must be remembering some of those yester-year stories that you have told me about. I hope I will live to be the age you are now, and can remember the pleasant things that happen to me, too. May God continue to bless you."

I didn't need to continue to thank her for her kind words because she so often said practically the same thing. But I did wave my hand

and give her a broad smile. If she were just coming in from work, many times I would invite her over to sit with me. Most of that time we would just sit, rock, and do very little talking. It was then that talking seemed to be too invasive into our privacy.

I was hoping that rocking would provide as much solace for her about her past as rocking provided for me, because I could still conjure up good memories about my Darden. When I thought about the depth of the love Darden had for me, I smiled. We had not yet been able to afford an automobile for transportation or pleasure, so we walked wherever we needed to go. There was still no public transportation available for the direction in which we were going.

Darden was always punctual, arriving home from his job at the manufacturing institute by six o'clock in the evening. I would hear a signal from the family pet, Prince, a German Shepherd. It sounded like an alto singing voice straining to reach the upper range of a first soprano voice. He would make this sound when Darden was only a block away from home. Prince was signaling the children, girls especially, that it was time for them to change out of their overalls into dresses. (Darden did not approve of females wearing pants.) The boys needed only to brush neat, straight parts in their hair, clean their dirty faces and blow any runny noses. (Darden would not tolerate snotty-nosed kids. Even if it were not his kid, he would offer a soft clean rag to a child, and order him to clean his nose.) I knew then I had to hurry to finish setting the supper table so that Darden and the family would be fed as soon as Darden had finished his own cleanup ritual.

Whether Darden came into the house upstairs through the front door of the split-level home, or entered downstairs through the kitchen door, if he didn't see me, his first words were, "Where's your Mother?" Always.

Darden was unrelenting about me working outside the home, especially because we now had four more children—Braxton, Cordice, Racina, and Neva. Darden felt I had more than just a few chores to do in keeping our home orderly, the laundry washed and ironed, and the family fed and clean. He did appreciate my efficiency as a housewife, and my overall dedication to my family. To show his love and appreciation, Darden purchased modern-day appliances, or other types of gadgetry that he thought might lighten my daily workload. Usually these things he made available for my birthday.

I wasn't always aware of when I was smiling, but my smiles mostly accompanied the good memories. Sometimes, though, If I lingered on any particular memory, my overall emotional behavior might change. You know, like sometimes I might begin to cry because I was having a negative feeling about one or another scenario.

Like now. It was in full ear range of all of our children. I had gone off to choir rehearsal, and had forgotten to turn off the oven of my new gas stove. The food I had placed in the warmer part of the oven had not burned. But, Darden was furious.

"You got your head set on doing everything for the church. You forgot you have full responsibilities right here at home. You could have burned up the food. Worse, caused a fire. You're nothing but an imbecile when it comes to your church!"

Normally, such harsh criticism from one person to another person suggests an underlying problem other than the one spoken of. I had not had reason to suspect Darden of any wrongdoing.

"Yes, I forgot." I thought I was keeping my voice calm and quiet. "But you got here in time to turn the oven off before anything major happened. What are you so bent out of shape about?"

"Bent out of shape! You're a real nitwit. There's just no talking to a dummy like you!" Darden stormed out of sight through the kitchen door.

No, that wasn't the only time that Darden had blown up at me. I had noticed that he found fault with me more and more over the years. All over something quite trivial. And I certainly didn't like for him to speak out so vehemently about my involvement in the church. His change in attitude created a curiosity in my mind—what was suspect about what I was doing? Or, was he trying to shift all attention away from himself because he was up to something no good?

There was a time, some ten years or so into our marriage, that presented itself as a serious problem. That problem became rather nasty.

Sometimes, in an effort to solidify new friendships, one might adopt a few habits of one's acquaintances. Darden had been working at this one job for a few years, but he had done little more than appear at work, cordially greet his co-workers, then work all day beside them in silence. He had practically no conversations with them. He did tire of his situation, and thought he should change.

Well, one day, at the invitation of a newcomer to the job, Darden ventured to accompany the newcomer and five others to a nearby beer parlor. Yes, more than just draft beer was served there, but Darden partook only of a draft beer. To him, the stuff tasted okay. That was his introduction to alcohol, and a different way of life.

Darden had not a clue that having more than one drink of beer was going to present itself as a negative in his life. Beer, besides affecting his sense of balance, wreaked havoc with his psyche. The first time he imbibed seemed to have encouraged a second time, and a third time. Then drinking became a habit. For a long, long time, Darden drank only beer.

The first time he came home smelling of beer, I made no comment. I knew the smell because my father and his brothers, and a few of their friends came together, frequently, at my father's home. They would sit, drink, and swap eccentric tales. Much of these times, before the men disbanded to return to their own homes, all of us children would have gone to bed and would be sound asleep. So, if there was unsteadiness in their walk, or muddling of their minds, we children were never aware. When, by chance, one of us saw a character wobbling down the street during the daytime, the talk was always that the person had been drinking moonshine, not beer. Not that we really knew the difference back then.

The first time Darden came home stumbling over and bumping into things, I was concerned and asked, "Are you all right?"

Well, I just should have kept my mouth shut. Darden exploded, "Who are you to come asking me things? It's my business what I do, and how I do it. Never you mind, you just do your thing."

Of course, by this time in my life, I just had to answer his remarks. "Have you forgotten that I'm your wife, and I have a right to know if you're all right or not? I was concerned about you, so be it."

"Look, woman, shut your mouth before I shut it for you!"

"What did you say? Ha! You and who else?"

Well, what did I say that for? He gave me a hard open-hand slap across my face. I screamed, waking the children, who then saw me cowering at the foot of my bed.

Almost in unison they asked, "Daddy, what did you do to Mama? Don't you hurt Mama!" They gathered protectively around me, flashing menacing looks at their father. Darden left the room and went to the kitchen. Soon, we all heard a sizzling noise and realized that he was cooking. The children did not yet know that Darden was unsteady afoot or mentally dishevelled because he had been drinking.

Over the next couple of weeks Darden regained his head long enough to realize he had been shucking his duty as sole provider for his family. He had been spending part of his weekly salary before he meted out the amounts necessary for me to take care of the household expenses. That part of his behavior changed. He began bringing home his weekly salary, giving it to me, and waiting for me to give him his allowance. An allowance is not what he called the portion of money that I returned to him for him to do with as he pleased. That's just what I called it, behind his back of course. I guessed correctly that he would continue to "join with the fellahs on the corner," and do whatever else they did. Sitting, drinking, and swapping tales, just like my father and family and friends had done years earlier. Perhaps I was a bit naive, but up to this time in our marriage, I had never entertained the idea that Darden could be "messing" around.

Shannon was now eleven and was having a great deal of difficulty adjusting to puberty. In my efforts to help her make the adjustment, I didn't exactly neglect any of my other children, but I did spend more quality time with Shannon.

Darden took advantage of the situation. He was easily persuaded by his peers, the very guys with whom he hung out on Saturday nights, to come along and enjoy the companionship of the few women who dared venture into their domain, their "on the corner" hangout.

There was one woman in particular who had set her sights on Darden. She had made all sorts of inquiries about him, so she was fully aware that he was a married man. Shucks! She didn't care. She wanted Darden for herself, and she wasn't going to let anything stop her from obtaining her goal. And Darden, poor thing, he didn't have a clue as to what was about to happen.

What did happen severely affected me. Darden began coming home later and later on Saturday nights, very disoriented. So much so that I knew some of his cronies had escorted him home, supporting his weight between them for the block and a half distance from their "on the corner" hangout. I usually pretended I was sound asleep.

Whether I was actually asleep, pretending to be asleep, or awake and up completing some preparation for church, Darden found some reason to attempt an argument. And if I happened to reply to anything he said, he would lambaste me for some ten or fifteen minutes, nonstop.

"You don't have sense enough to know your foot from your behind. I've never known anyone so dumb. Where did you come from anyway? Don't you turn away when I'm talking to you. Look at you. You don't even know how to comb your own hair. Who else do you know parts their hair in the middle of the head? Looks like a road opening up to the doodoo pot. Ha. Ha. That's your brain, you know."

I sincerely hoped that none of what he said held any true meaning, that it was the alcohol talking and not him. He continued.

"I had to teach you everything you know. Ole dumb ass thang. Yeah, thang! When I look at you, sometimes I want to puke. Yeah, you make me sick. Go outta my sight, old woman. I don't like looking at stupid people. Stupid, like you."

Somewhere in the maze of those epithets that Darden hurled at me, I lost my self-confidence. So, again, I turned to the church for consolation. But I never neglected my family in spite of what Darden believed. Getting more involved with the church, this time, meant serving on the usher board every first Sunday, and singing in the Senior Choir the second and fourth Sundays.

One thing I knew about myself that Darden was ineffective in shattering my confidence about, was I could read. I set out to broaden my horizon by reading as much as I could. The school books that our children brought home from school provided a great deal of reading. When one needed to use the colored public library to complete a school assignment, I and all of the children went to the library. I even got very interested in doing arithmetic along with the children. They believed that I was helping them with their homework. What I was doing was learning right along with them.

I ended my busy days with a few verses I would read from the Bible. And I tried to assure God, imagine, that I was not going to let anything Darden hurled at me during his disoriented rampages get under my skin. Of course, I did believe that was going to be the hardest job I had ever undertaken. Darden had been so cruel. I had to learn the reason why.

Wouldn't you know it, the devil was let loose. The conniving female, with her devil wish to destroy my family by taking away my children's father and my husband, put her plan into action when she planted a kiss on his cheek and smudged his shirt collar. She had only to wait a week to get some reaction to her lipstick smudge.

Yes, I saw the smudge on wash day, but I didn't react to it in the manner the hussy guessed. Instead, I called my closest friend, Pectola. Pectola kept up with the happenings around town in that she worked out and among the general public. I wouldn't have to tell Pecky a thing. She began most of our meetings by telling me what the latest scuttlebutt around town was. All the while, Darden continued being severely insensitive to me.

Now, according to him, I wasn't ironing his shirts correctly. He also insisted that I press his undershorts, fold them a certain way (he changed the folding pattern each week), and hang his shirts on hangers instead of folding them as would be done in a laundry.

Pectola had heard the scuttlebutt that Darden was "involved." What to do? She didn't want to tell me, but she felt I should know. She didn't want to do or say anything that could interrupt our very close friendship.

After giving it serious thought, Pecky told me this story, "Girl, I heard that some females have been showing up, of late, at several of the guys' hangouts. I didn't hear which hangouts, but my guess is, if they frequented one, they browsed into them all. And I heard that these girls were out for one thing—*married men.*"

"Are any of these women married?"

"The way I heard it, my guess is they are not."

"Then why would they want to interfere in a married man's life?"

"Come on, get with it, Leanna. A married man is not gonna want to be fathering two and three families. So, the females figure they can have their fun, yet not have the same kind of worry about having children that a wife would have."

"But, Pecky, you and I know better. I heard a couple of years ago that Maizell's husband had an affair, and he had a child by his mistress."

You know without me having to tell you that this conversation was in no way helping to boost my self-confidence. And about my own predicament, my decision was to intensify my faith in God. Over the years, I had gleaned from all those Sunday services that, "God the Father is with you always. Just believe in Him. And trust in Him." I promised myself that I would put more trust in Him. As another means of actively participating in the ongoing activities at my church, I decided that I would invite the pastor to my home for a Saturday evening meal, just as many of the choir members were doing. But I didn't have a clue that what I was about to undertake would only make my situation with Darden much worse.

The very first time my pastor appeared at our home for a Saturday evening meal, Darden returned home to gather something he had forgotten to take with him on his free time out. Reverend Franc Barton, who had been seated at the set dinner table, got an eyeful and earful of Darden Swelton.

"So, you're the pastor of Shands Methodist Church. Well, didn't anyone ever tell you that *my* children get fed first; then, if there is anything left over, the grownups can have at it? I don't mind you coming here. Just know, you don't take food out of *my* children's mouths." Darden left the house.

I began calling each child to the table. I was fiercely holding back tears of shame. I was ashamed of Darden's attitude. Reverend Barton agreed that the children should be fed first, and they were. Then Reverend Barton and I ate our meal.

The pastor became a frequent visitor, but not to eat. His intent was to meet with Darden and persuade him to visit at his church. Darden always managed to dodge him. Darden was very angry with me as he thought it was my doing to get the pastor to seek him out. And the angrier Darden got, the more insults he hurled at me.

I was vaulted into the present time when I pulled at the sleeve of my blouse and tore it. I fussed at myself. "Why didn't I assert myself?" I must have thought that fiddling with my blouse, buttoning and unbuttoning it, then straightening its collar, would somehow mend the sleeve I had just torn. I kept fussing with myself. "Why didn't I make a few decisions totally on my own? Now, now, stop fretting. God has stepped into each of my unhappy situations in His own time, and I can't say that I could have improved on any of the end results."

I jolted my head twice, sat staring straight ahead, unseeing, before I could return to the realm of the past years. I remembered a plan that Darden and I had used on the children. If a child wanted to do a certain thing or go somewhere out of the ordinary, Darden and I invariably directed that child to each other. What we said was, "Go ask your father." Or, "Go ask your mother." When the child realized he or she had been turned away from both Darden and myself in that manner, well, there would be no further discussion. Mind you, neither Darden nor I figured that solving a situation was the best way to handle it, but so far it was effective for us. Every day, we were learning a great deal about parental responsibilities.

The sky began to cloud over, and I saw lightning and heard thunder in the distance. I got up out of my porch rocker and rested its high back forward against the house. Usually, if there were high winds accompanying a darkening sky, the chairs on the porch got bounced around and I didn't want to lose even one out into the yard. I went into the house, closed the front door, and decided I'd go take a short nap. I felt a bit sleepy.

Sleep was too long in coming, so I got up again. These tired, old, out-of-focus eyes slowly scanned that wall in the living room that was the backside of the kitchen wall. I didn't see a single picture that hung there. More and more I seemed not to be seeing things that occupied the space in the direction in which my head was turned. I seated myself in the sculptured gold velvet chair, showing much wear now, that was squarely rooted by the opened front door.

Slowly, back and forth, up and down, my eyes passed over the pictures hanging on that one wall, but I saw not one. I turned my attention to the street when I heard the public city bus droning down the street past the house. School kids chattered noisily with each other as they walked past the house. Sometimes, when I felt aroused and cheerful, or for any reason whatever, I would mosey out the door onto the front porch and sit in my rocking chair and greet the children as they passed en route to their homes from perhaps a busy school day.

Though I couldn't remember any child's name, I was reminded of how my own children had skipped, jumped, strolled, and chattered when going to and coming from school. I had loved having some little treats waiting for them when they arrived home. Sometimes I had baked sweet potatoes, sometimes roasted ears of corn, and sometimes other things that they particularly liked.

I must have been laughing out loud when my neighbor got out of her parked car and walked toward her front porch because she waved as she flashed me a toothy grin. I didn't feel embarrassed. I know I'm advancing in age, and I realize that much of the time I'm here alone with so little left by my children for me to do, so I entertain myself any way I can.

At that particular moment I remembered that Darden would "order" everyone back to the kitchen about eight o'clock each weekday evening. They were "ordered" to come to hear some far-fetched yarns that Darden liked to spin. And sometimes, just sometimes, Darden would be fictionalizing the truth, usually about one or more of our children. We would top off the evening meal with a light snack— maybe lemonade and cookies, or popcorn that we had grown in our own garden, or maybe just have some homemade ice cream.

On one such evening, the youngest of our children, Neva, removed herself from her perch at the top of the stairs that led from the kitchen up to the second floor. Silently, she wandered into the bedroom that could be reached only by traveling through the living room or the clothes closet. Clumsily, she leaned backward against the bed, and fell sound asleep with only the back of her head resting on top of the mattress. She had left so quietly that she was not missed until the story was told, then a frantic search was begun to find her. We were yelling and calling her name, which did not disturb her sleep. When she was found in that peculiar but funny pose, it was a joyous moment to behold. After that incident, Darden began holding his family sessions a half-hour earlier as he liked capturing the attention of all the family members.

Alone on my porch rocking back and forth, and watching the school children trafficking past my house, I was suddenly longing to be free, again! Sometimes, I thought I understood what it would mean to be free, but almost as quickly as the thought occurred, it would elude my attempt at perusal.

CHAPTER 6

▼

HEAD MUSIC

As each one of the children reached an age of understanding equal to the level of an adult, Darden's philosophical teachings became subtle. He believed in ingenuity. He wanted the children to be fully aware of the Ten Commandments, and to accept them in their own ways.

Whenever there was a gathering of the children, especially on a rainy day when all there was to do was sit around and talk, Darden might overhear some of their conversations. Their conversations sometimes included negative comments about an individual not a part of our family, or a situation not relative to our way of life. Whenever this occurred Darden would pass through the room and pause long enough to ask the children such a question as, "Were you there?" Or maybe, "Did you witness it?" If the answer that he heard was, "No," Darden would be certain to continue passing through, exiting the room with the comment, "Then what'cha talkin' 'bout it for?"

One would think that if you heard the same message more than once or twice, and certainly a third time, one would begin a deductive process to determine what the message meant. I often wondered if any child other than Maida had figured out what their father staunchly believed in. And that Maida had figured out his message was a pleasant surprise. You see, I had been seeing Maida as my "slow" child, because no matter what her encounter, she did not stop backing away from all confrontations until she reached high school. Even with her own siblings.

Pectola, my best friend, stopped in for a visit late one Saturday afternoon. I suggested we occupy the front porch swing where we could swing low forcing the weighted swing to pull hard against the ceiling hooks which made noisy squeaks. I made that suggestion because Pectola wore a facial expression that said, "Girl, I have something juicy to tell you." And, if we sat there, no one could hear our conversation unless one was sitting right there with us. You would have thought we were mere teenagers whenever the two of us got together, such giggling and snickering going on.

Right away I sensed it must have been about someone we both knew well. It was.

She began, "Your neighbor, girl, just lost another beau. She just can't figure out the right thing to do with any man."

"Are you going to talk about Janiece?"

"So, who else around here dips snuff? Of course. And if you'll shut up, I'll get on with my tale." She paused to await silence. "Wednesday before last, Janiece was expecting her fella to call at her home about seven o'clock. That same day she did some volunteer services for the Salvation Army. She worked later than she had intended, so didn't get home in time to spiffy up her house to receive her gentleman caller. You know what I mean, like clean out her spittoon, for one thing. Well, the fella arrived, and was shown into the parlor. That day, he opted to occupy the chair in which Janiece usually sat, but he didn't notice her spittoon.

"You know how nervous Janiece can get around men. Well, this day was no exception. When she entered the room, she tried to be light on her feet—you know, do that dainty walking. She wanted to cross in front of her fella to the chair beyond. Well, waa-laa, it happened! She tripped over a pucker in the throw rug. As she fell forward, she threw her hands out in front of herself expecting to break her fall. One hand did, for it actually caught the top side of the spittoon and flipped it over, and most of that yuckey brown liquid inside it splattered all over the pant legs and shoes of her male friend.

"Needless to say, that incident ended her newest relationship. And girl, Janiece herself told Sarah about the whole thing. Well, if Sarah lets the story fly and the grapevine picks it up, girl, watch out! I honestly feel sorry for Janiece. She is really a very nice person. Sarah said Janiece told her that one incident cured her of dipping snuff."

"Yeah, right, this I gotta see. I also think Janiece is a nice person. I hope, and soon, that she will find a suitable and lasting companion. She deserves a good man."

At that very moment in my peripheral vision, I caught sight of Darden standing at the open window of the bedroom that was directly opposite of where we sat swinging. I have to admit that a flood of guilt coursed through my body for I just knew that Darden had heard the two of us gossiping. Darden didn't approve of gossiping, and it didn't matter that you might consider the gossip good.

Just as quickly as I had flushed with guilt that we might have been heard, I tossed the notion of adhering to Darden's rules right out the window. How dare he try to police my conversations, I'm not his child. Oh, wow, what feisty thoughts can rule your head when you think you've gotten caught in a dirty deed. I felt guilty anyway because it could just as easily have been one of the children who had been standing there by that window and heard us talking. My mind froze. It probably took me a number of seconds to thaw back to normalcy. I resolved that instant that if Darden dared speak about gossiping to me, I'd simply say, "You had no business trying to hear."

I wonder why it is so hard for me to get out of my nightgown and housecoat before it gets to be noon any day. While I'm sitting here in this old gold chair tugging at my gown, my brain is playing tug of war with rights and wrongs. "Why can't people just be what they want to be without somebody putting limits on what they can do, on where they can go, and on what they can say?" I must be imagining that I'm talking to Darden.

Oh, shucks, now I've gone and torn my gown. "Darden, see what you made me do? You had no business listening. I was talking to Pectola. Oh, forget it."

My yesteryear and my today have overlapped because I'm visiting in two time slots which feels like I'm in the same orbit. I really need to pull myself together and get a grip on what seems to be happening to me these days. I hear myself sometimes talking out loud to myself, and sometimes I'm talking out loud to Darden. My God, I *know* Darden is dead, and buried.

Darden and I didn't really have many verbal disagreements. But if we did, they were some doozies. But of course, that was early on in our marriage when some of the children were still quite young. It took me a few days to get over one of those hurtful disagreements, because I always felt that Darden got the upper hand and won the argument.

Our children were, as most children, very perceptive. They knew when there was discord between their father and me, even if they had heard no discussions. I'll tell you why. Darden and I had this togetherness thing where we did a little something extra special for each other. My specialty for Darden was, once a week, giving his feet a complete pedicure. Because he did not own a car and had to walk to his every destination, at the end of every week his feet were ready to be treated with something special. Only I seemed capable of giving that special soothing.

But, oh boy, if there had been a disagreement or two during the week that really upset me, I would "punish" Darden by purposely neglecting to give him his much needed pedicure. The children would see him walking gingerly for a few days, and that was how they knew there had been some discord. Of course, the children thought it very funny to see Darden walking that way, but they never let him catch them laughing at his situation.

Darden's something special for me was a small box of my favorite chocolates, or cookies, or maybe a separate quarter-pound bag of my favorite nuts. The children always got a treat on Fridays. Usually theirs was penny-priced peanut butter logs, or a pound of Spanish peanuts. And I was called upon to create their favorite cookies.

Of course, if I had found reason not to give Darden his weekly pedicure, he would in return withhold his special something from me for that week. We would have one of those tit-for-tat situations going on.

I recall having a very strange experience about seven years after Darden first revealed that there was a demonic side to himself.

In this experience I thought I heard music and turned my head in the direction the music seemed to have been coming from. I saw nothing that might have been producing the music, but I was so certain that music was what I heard. When Larson entered the room, I asked him where the music was coming from.

Larson replied, "Mother, I don't hear anything."

Nearly everyday I continued to hear this music. And though it was very calming to me, I was unable to identify where it was coming from. For a rather lengthy period of time I felt mostly frightened, then I felt pleased, and next I resigned myself to believing I was losing my mind. Suddenly, I knew the music was of myself, made by myself, calming to myself, and saving of myself.

"Yes, Lord, yes! I hear the music in my head!" No one of the tunes had names. No name was needed. I *knew* each tune was God! My Redeemer! God had come to set me free!

So, thereafter, whenever Darden lashed out at me with his verbal abuse, the music started up in my head. No, the music did not completely plug up my ears, but it sure softened the blow of the abuse Darden exhaled at me.

And, something happened to Darden only a few weeks after the music revelation to me. Apparently, Darden had begun closure on his relations outside of the home. His nights out were fewer and shorter. There was no more evidence that he was drinking beer. He did admit to an occasional drink of an alcoholic beverage, like vodka, or gin. His temperament toward me dramatically softened. His pals frequented our home less often, and they ceased playing cards in our home. One would have thought that Darden had gotten religion. Or maybe, that Darden had returned to his early religious teachings.

So now, I'm making an emphatic statement that Darden the husband related to Leanna the wife (me) as lovingly as when we first began our life as a couple. My worth to Darden had resurfaced. I was like a disease to him, but a disease that he couldn't bear to be rid of.

CHAPTER 7

▼

CONVERSATIONS WITH HERSELF

Much of the time when I'm having thoughts about my family, I'm unaware that I talk to myself, aloud.

"What's happened to the birds? I don't hear them singing their beautiful songs. Who took away my fragrant flowers?" Occasionally, I'm tuned in to the fact that such thoughts as these have been haunting me for a few years. I just don't know why.

I don't think that I told you when it was that Racina made her permanent move into my home. It was two and a half years after Darden died. I overheard her tell one of her sisters one day that she was going to be taking care of me, as I shouldn't be living by myself anymore.

"I've been at this living alone ever since Darden died and haven't needed anyone to help me do whatever I have wanted to do. What makes any one of my children think that I need them now?" Of course, you know that I've long known about the discord between Racina and her husband, and that the discord hasn't been all verbal. The physical abuse began only a few years back, but she needed to have gotten out of there before now. Racina had talked once about filing for divorce, but I haven't heard anything further. So you see, I think Racina is using this move into my home "to look after Mother to the best of my ability" as a means of escaping her own home situation.

None of the other children objected to Racina's move. In fact they thought it the best move to get away from her husband's abuse. Strange that no one thought to ask my permission first. No, I wouldn't have turned her down. She is my daughter. But, I do have a right to my own privacy!

Well sir, right away Racina began to do almost every task that I set out to do. She must have meant for this busy work to be therapy for herself, but she overdid it! Wasn't long before I realized that I wasn't doing any of my usual house chores. Even my cooking possibilities had been tampered with. I'd turn on my electric stove and *nothing* would happen! I had deep thoughts and concluded, "So this is what was meant by 'look after Mother to the best of my ability.'"

I noticed a subtle change in the attitudes of some of the children which went unnoticed by Racina. Unnoticed until one of them voiced an opinion.

"Mama would be better off in a nursing facility. There she would be fed at regular times. She would be medicated properly when or if she so needed. You know, taking care of the infirm is their job."

I could almost see the wheels spinning in Racina's head, like out of control, at the many possibilities that would open up for her. By this time in her life, she had very few friends left, all because she had chosen to take her husband's abusive guff for so long. Momentarily those thoughts invaded Racina's head until a space clearance revealed not one of her siblings had also volunteered to look after their mother to the best of their ability.

But then everyone began acting guilty for having entertained the thoughts about a nursing home in the first place. And for at least another year after that initial nursing home idea, each sibling continued the treks to do chores "for Mama" that gave each some moral satisfaction.

But they did not know! They were repeating the same chores they had begrudgingly performed years and years ago. Only now, I was not assigning any child a chore that had to be completed before his or her scheduled bedtime.

At my age now, eighty-eight, I know I am not sharp enough to perceive differences in the attitudes of my children or the seriousness of their intentions. I just believe that it is sheer love that each child holds for me, nothing more and nothing less.

I suspect that Racina is very aware of the differences in the attitudes of her siblings who come over here to do "things" for me. I'm basing my suspicion on the fact that now the conversations between them and Racina are brief. Even Cordice, with whom she has always been closest, has brief conversations during her week-long visits that have been reduced to three times a year.

Previously during groupings here, they would all laugh heartily for hours, even bellow comments from room to room, as they busied themselves with their chosen chores to "help" me. But not now. Like when Cordice arrives, she hurriedly completes the usual amenities, then busys herself reorganizing my linen closet. At the hint of conversation beyond the amenities, Cordice might begin whistling, or softly singing, anything to have an excuse for not having heard Racina speaking to her. It took more effort to avoid conversation than Cordice imagined. Many times she even picked up a magazine, a tabloid, or True Confessions, but never a good book, and "read" for hours.

That was when Racina paid attention. That Cordice never liked to read anything was plenty of cause for Racina to wonder if something was wrong with her sister.

Racina questioned, "Cordice, what have you and Eddie been up to lately?"

Cordice managed to get through the week revealing little about herself and her husband.

"Racina, you remember Debra, she lives down the street from me?"

"Yeah."

"Well, she and I went to this Tupperware party last week, and when we left there, we stopped in Lentera's Department Store. We saw some fabulous fashions, all new for this fall. I can't wait to get back there and buy myself an outfit or two. Are you coming up this year to do your shopping?"

"I'm not often able to get away, you know. If I see a way, perhaps, I will come."

When Cordice used such off-the-wall tactics with Racina to stifle further curiosity about herself and Eddie, it gave Racina reason to immediately suspect trouble in Cordice's marriage. Racina asked no more personal questions of her sister Cordice.

Neva's attentiveness to me was perhaps the easiest, for she used her children as her excuse to hurry in and out of my house. I can't recall hearing Neva refer to her children as nearly out of control. But, Darden had lovingly made reference to those grandchildren as "unruly citizens" only in my presence. Earlier, he had witnessed how they competed with each other while vying for parental attention. Since Neva mainly taxied me from place to place, she simply reduced the number of times that she made appearances.

I'm almost certain that none of the children ever thought that I could hear any parts of their conversations with each other. Occasionally I did hear bits and pieces, enough to know they were discussing a fate for me.

Larson to Braxton, "Braxton, what are your feelings about placing Mom in a long-term care facility?"

"Oh, I don't know. Sometimes I think Mom would get good and constant care if she were being cared for by trained personnel. But, can you put any real trust in those places with hopes that they will do the right thing for those in their custody?"

I heard Neva and Maida each express similar sentiments, but Maida had even more to say.

"I have been hearing and seeing some horrific things about nursing homes, and I don't want to go that route. At least not until there are laws passed to protect the residents in such places. I know the nursing homes are not all alike, but how do you choose the right one?"

I do have to say that when I overheard my children discussing putting me in a nursing home, I became frightened. My mind raced back to moments shortly after Darden died. My brain scrambled furiously to sort out and put some order to anything and everything that I could have done, or said, that would have my children entertaining ideas of putting me away. "Away" is the gist of putting someone into a nursing home. No one plans to come visiting often enough to suggest that they really love you. One really becomes a "lost" soul. That is not for me is what I began and continued telling myself.

"Surely, my children have to believe, no, they have to *know* that there is nothing wrong with me. So what if I forget something a time or two. Doesn't everyone experience forgetfulness? I even heard my children mention *senility*. And *alteim*, uh, *elhime*, oh whatever it is. But they don't, no, they aren't, well, I just won't believe this. They're beginning to treat me like I'm the daughter and they're the mother."

For sometime now, I've been acting like a horse champing at the bit, storming out of my bedroom and down the hall, spinning around on my heels then retracing my steps, and all the while I'm forcibly exhaling my breath through gritted teeth. Suddenly, I realized the reason for my actions—my children have removed even my paring knives. Now, darn it, I can't even peel an apple for myself. Confound it, they've put an end to the simplest of my tasks. I have tried agreeing with each one who has disagreed with me over something I've said or done, which would have been something trivial in my mind, but that has seemed to work less in my favor than to simply let them always contradict me. Doggone it, now I have to guard every word I speak to any one of them.

"I'm not going to let them put me anywhere except right where I am—in my own home! Some nerve!" I guess I just haven't been "with it" enough to realize that there is a concerted conspiracy against me.

For the longest kind of time Racina has acted like she was cleverly disguising her intrusiveness on my daily routines especially when she opted to treat me to a coffee-house breakfast two or three times a week. Or maybe treat me to lunches at The Dugout. Sometimes, she even reversed the whole procedure and prepared the meals by herself leaving the table settings for me to take care of.

"Racina, you're bugging me now. What, prey tell, is wrong with me cooking us breakfast and lunch, and even dinner?" I know I asked her that same question more than just a few times, until I got tired of hearing it myself.

"Oh, Mother, I'm just trying to make things easier for you. At your age, I would think you'd welcome someone doing things for you."

"Well, just thank you much, Missy. But I'm quite capable of doing those things by myself."

"Yeah, right, I know." That was a snide remark she just made. I've stopped getting any respect these days.

"Well, if you didn't know before, you certainly ought to know by now. Just what did you do to my stove? When I turn a burner on, nothing happens."

Racina ignored my question, and that's what I mean when I say I don't get any respect anymore. But I didn't stop there with my questions.

"When I ask someone to do something for me and they oblige, sure, I'm very thankful. But, when have I asked any one of you for help? I know I don't hear myself asking anyone. And, as long as I have my good health I won't ask. And even you can't say that I don't have my good health."

"Just chalk it up to me, Mama. I'm enjoying doing things for you for a change. Okay?" That reply was surely a peppered one.

Racina had really upended my usual and daily activities to the extent that even my kitchen knives were "misplaced." It had taken her just two months after moving into my home to create such chaos for me. I felt I was only a few steps away from being an invalid. I began asking of myself, "Leanna, have you done something, something very wrong?" When I was unable to fathom a sensible answer, I would ask Racina about the "takeover" of my home, especially my kitchen.

You guessed right; I usually got no reply from Racina. Being that frustrated, I often left the kitchen in a huff, maybe even jerking my head from right to left, and scolding her with my pet expression, "tsk," in utter disgust.

Strange, but I do realize that educated people know so much that they really don't know squat. My meaning is meant to address all the experts who say that "exercise is good for everyone." I do agree, to a point. What I wonder is why persons intending to "care" for someone's well-being, right away heap their own personal routines upon their "patients?" The total effect is that the "patient" is stripped of his own personal desires. Personally, I think that is the fastest and subtlest way to force a person into poor health, whether it is mental, moral, or physical!!

Back to my relationship with Racina. One day, I chose to ask, "Racina, why do you always want to eat out?"

Her hostile reply, "Because nobody has to go in the kitchen and worry about what to cook, for one reason."

"And for what other reason?" My words and tone were equally as hostile.

"Mama, you're starting to annoy me with all your questioning of my every move. Can't you just sit back and enjoy someone else doing the work for a change? Jeez!" And she slammed shut a kitchen cabinet door.

Well, to that attitude, I stormed into the living room and landed myself in my favorite plush chair planted by the front door, and stared menacingly at the opening into the kitchen where Racina was working. I wasn't sure at that moment if I wanted Racina to appear in that doorway, for I just might speak something to her that was rather unseemly. I remember I crossed my legs at the knees and began bouncing one leg above the other, and started humming aloud one of my no-name tunes always present in my head. It was about fifteen minutes and I was calmed down. Other times when Racina so upset me, I would start fussing with my silk flowers, rearranging and then dabbing rose oil on the rose petals. The smell of roses was soothing to my discomfort. "No one is going to stop me from smelling the flowers! So there!"

Calm now, I left my chair and went through the kitchen and out onto the back stoop and stood looking at the houses and yards on the next street. It looked to me that the plum tree in the Minards' yard had been seriously infested with maybe some boring insects, as no fruit had yet appeared for the season. Oh, and Mrs. Calahan's petunia beds, which flanked the entrance walk up to their house, provided the entire neighborhood with luxuriant color. "Gee, they must have a straight pipeline to God because they continue to have the prettiest flowers in the area. Yeah, we all get out here and try to help nature along, but they are the ones with the most success." I forgot to tell you that sometimes I talk out loud to myself and answer to no one except myself.

I wandered from the stoop out into my own yard, traveling from bed to bed, examining the flowers. When I got to the apple tree I looked up and saw there probably would be a bumper crop. My apples are always good, at least, when the neighborhood children and the school children passing by let them do their ripening on the tree. We'd never objected to the children partaking of the fruit as long as they asked permission first. Most did, and I continued to permit.

By the time I got to the door of the storage shed, I faltered for a moment as I heard myself speaking to Darden, "Daddy, bring that thinning fork out after you've settled the mower in place. I think I'll transfer some of these verbena to the corner of the house on the east side."

I was just short of being flabbergasted as I couldn't believe myself. "Am I losing my mind? I know Darden is dead. He's been dead all of four years now. What is wrong with me?"

I thought I would be safer inside the house if I was going to be talking to my Darden, so I continued around the side of the house to the front door, but I decided to sit in my rocking chair on the porch for a short while, instead. I yet didn't want to speak to Racina. And you know what happened next. Yep, the rocking triggered pleasant thoughts about my Darden, and I sure didn't mind.

"I'm okay. I just needed to sit here for awhile." And I allowed myself to be amused by my thoughts.

I had spent six weeks planning a surprise birthday party for Darden. "You men always claim you cannot be surprised. Well, I'll bet if I tried I could pull a surprise on you." I was exhibiting a wide grin, but behind his back. Right away I got the kids involved in my scheme to effect the surprise. Maida wanted to tackle making a coverall for our old and worn sofa.

Maida was only seventeen at the time and I believed that she could do the job so I gave her the money to buy the yard goods, and then told her to make sure that she left no evidence around that her father might catch sight of. Now, I had taught each of my daughters to sew, and had even taught my sons the basics. Only Shannon and Maida had continued a real interest in sewing, with Maida's interest branching out to things other than just clothes. In fact, Maida easily learned other sewing techniques, like tatting, knitting, crocheting, and the like.

We secured the Community Activity Hall as the best suited place for the surprise party. My sons delivered the invitations and cautioned each guest to keep the surprise a real surprise.

I had asked Stanford Lang for help. He had a car. So, on the appointed evening for the event, Stanford suggested that Darden and he make a quick stop at The Juicer—the newest "spirits" joint—for a beer or two in celebration of Darden's birthday. Darden accepted and they drove off the company lot in the direction of The Juicer. Stanford's task was to lure Darden into Community Activity Hall on the pretense he needed help in bringing some stuff home for his wife. That way he'd only have to make one trip inside. Darden obliged.

Of course, Darden told all of his adult guests that he wasn't surprised. Well, maybe he wasn't at the hall, but what he had not figured
on was yet to come. The real surprise awaited him at home.

When the party was over, everyone left the hall in a jovial mood.
We traveled home in a taxi, as we yet did not own a car. Darden
opened the front door and truly got the surprise of his life—there
stood Caesar, his older brother, from whom there had been no word
for years. (The children had let him into the home after seeing his face
and hearing his voice tell of his whereabouts over the years. They concluded there was no mistaking him being their father's "long lost"
brother.)

Mind you, Caesar was not our planned surprise, but he turned out
to be a happy surprise for all of us. That surprise almost overshadowed
the planned one, Samuel, Darden's very best friend from when he lived
in Cayuga. Darden was further flabbergasted when he noticed how we
had spruced up the house.

And Darden had always boasted, "No one can pull a surprise on
me." Ha! Got'cha, this time.

I left my rocking chair and went into the house to make a few phone
calls to the children who lived out of state. I found what I thought was
Maida's current address and phone number, and began dialing. I
punched in seven numbers on the telephone but got an abrupt message
from someone on the other end.

"We're sorry, but your call cannot go through. If this is a long distance call, please hang up then try your call again."

I hung up the phone, looked at the number in my address book,
then dialed the number again. I knew I had the correct number but I
was forgetting that I had to dial the number "1" followed by the
three-digit area code number. So no matter that I had the last seven
numbers correct, I was not going to be able to reach Maida without
some dialing assistance. Racina had walked down to a neighbor's
house, but I wouldn't have asked her for help had she been there in the

house. Yes, I was still upset with her. My stroll around the house, and my porch-rocking, back-home-in-Cayuga memories had not sufficiently eased my anger at Racina.

Every day, as soon as Racina arrived home from work, she would start in on me about not having any radio or television turned on. You guessed it, all semblance of sanity would leave my mind.

"Racina, I'm gonna tell you once more. When I want to hear that noise, I'll turn on the radio. Or, I'll turn on the TV. I don't want either on now. Do you understand me?" I was close to screaming those words at Racina.

"There you go again, Mama, insisting that nobody can do anything that's right for you."

Despite my protests, Racina would turn one or the other on, and turn it up to her own desired volume. Racina was still young enough for loud, of course. I took that to mean she had *no* regard for my feelings.

One particular day the radio was so loud, I remember that I left the room and went down the hall to the bathroom. I couldn't get control of my emotions and found myself sobbing into my bath towel hoping that Racina couldn't hear me. Her actions had to be deliberate defiance.

I recovered control long enough to leave the bathroom, and go to my bedroom. I sat on the side of the bed and tried hard to think rationally. I wondered if I had lost *all* control of my very own domain. Was there anything to be done short of ordering Racina out of my home? I really didn't want to do that. My home is the likely place for Racina because I have the space. But I can't let her take over, as it appears is the current situation. I must do something pronto. Just how do I put a halt to Racina's progressive takeover?

Racina has been a spitfire for most of her life, but that is no reason for her to treat me now as if she is at the same age level as I am.

Ashton and Racina's marriage became stormy almost from its beginning. Those two had not known each other long enough to realize that their relationship was little more than physical attraction. Before long, they wore on each others nerves over most any subject. The arguments over money were the most troubling. Ashton would leave the house whenever it appeared Racina was winning an argument. She never did understand that it was she who drove him into the arms of the other woman with her constant nit-picking.

After a few years of arguing and taking longer and longer to stimulate their once passionate physical attraction to each other, Ashton became physically abusive. Then was when Racina began her late afternoon visits with me. She would stay long enough for Ashton, an early riser, to have retired to bed and fallen asleep. Then she wouldn't have to have any conversations with him at all. After almost two years of this routine, Ashton announced he was filing for divorce. It became final three months after Racina moved in with me.

During the last three years that Racina remained with Ashton, many of their friends sought and made new friends with persons more compatible. No matter that Racina was now on her own, she was unsuccessful in rejuvenating any friendships of previous years. Having no social interaction with any of her peers, and having been practically deserted by her siblings with any "help with Mama" made for a rather bitter Racina. She felt she had reason to do anything she wanted. "Lord have mercy on anyone who gets in my way," became her attitude, and anyone did include me, Leanna, her mother.

The children had to have doctored my cooking appliances so that I couldn't operate them whenever I had food that needed cooking. I started making sure that when we shopped for groceries, I bought enough fruit and cottage cheese to be available for my lunch meals. Racina had long since taken over the task of preparing breakfast and dinner, but too often forgot that I, the homebody, needed lunch same as she did.

For as long as the weather was warm, I would escape all of life's challenges by sitting in my rocking chair on my front porch. Though it was never purposely done, it always happened that I would begin to remember things about our lives that happened so many years ago.

I was having thoughts now of how protective Darden was of our girls to keep them away from the wrong kind of boys. Also protective of the boys to keep them from straying down the wrong path.

Because our home was not yet equipped with a telephone line, Darden relied on word of mouth from interested persons in the community for "hot" news. One day Maida visited her girlfriend, Eliza, who lived four long blocks away. When she arrived at the home of her friend, there was another girlfriend also visiting. This girl lived a considerable distance further than Maida, so she had to begin her return home earlier than Maida needed to, in order to arrive home before dark. It was a custom of these young girls to "walk piece the way home" with the visiting friend. That is what Maida and Eliza chose to do this particular Sunday. En route, they reached a major highway they needed to cross. Maida, being the slowest of the three, chose not to speed up and try to outrun the approaching car, but rather to wait at the curbing until it passed. None of the three girls had noticed a young man to their rear heading in their same direction, until the young man stopped alongside Maida, and likewise waited for the car to pass. Maida and he spoke, for they knew each other from school, and they continued on across the highway. Maida and Eliza chose not to go further with Kayla, but to say their so longs right there. Justin, the young man, chose to pause long enough to also speak to Eliza and Kayla before continuing on his way.

Well! Some busybody misinterpreted the happenstance meeting and quickly routed a message to Darden that his daughter was meeting young boys on street corners! By the time Maida left Eliza at her "piece the way home" point and arrived home, she was met by Darden who ushered her to the kitchen for a private consultation.

"Just what do you mean, young lady, meeting boys on the street corner?"

"Daddy," she started.

Maida tried to give her father a truthful reply, but he was so furious that one of his girls had defied his rules that she never got to say more than just his name. He stalked her with his words, "How dare you pretend to be visiting with your friends when what you're doing is meeting boys on street corners!"

Maida stuttered more than once, but Darden's ranting and raving gave her no opportunity to sandwich in more than a single word. Poor Maida. She was allowed to leave the room after she could no longer hold back the tears. To Darden, this was a kind of defiance. But he knew he needed only to speak to get her full attention.

Maida told me what had actually happened, then asked who could have been watching them to conjure up such a vicious lie. I turned out to be her very best friend, for I listened to her truth. I held her in my arms until she had calmed, and I didn't even have to say anything.

Darden did not deny Maida future opportunities to go places after that. Maida did, on one occasion, catch a glimpse of Darden browsing in the same general area as herself. She didn't have to wonder why. She would be a young adult before Darden would focus his watchful eyes on his three daughters younger than Maida.

Shannon, our oldest, had already graduated from high school and traveled up the east coast to Vermont to be with Darden's youngest cousin while in pursuit of a job. Not only did Shannon find employment almost immediately after arriving in Vermont, but she met a young man who captured her heart. He asked her to marry him after knowing each other only three months. After conferring with his cousin, who was expected to scrutinize this young man as if he were asking to marry a daughter of his, Darden gave his consent for Shannon to marry. So, at the ripe old age of nineteen, Shannon became a married woman and no longer had to answer to Darden about anything.

I had paid attention to Shannon's plight while she was at home, but only after I realized that each time Shannon wanted to go to the movies with her girlfriends or do anything with them that was away from the house, Darden had insisted that she take Maida along too. It was a few years before Maida revealed to me that Shannon sometimes did meet with a young man. Supposedly, he was the apple of her eye during her high school years. Maida told me she had let him bribe her into keeping quiet about those meetings, mainly because she liked his looks and liked him even more because he usually gave her a dime as a bribe. That dime, to Maida, was a rich man's bribe. Of course, the bribe would get spent before she returned home. I guffawed with laughter when I remembered that Maida had suffered stomachaches many times after "chaperoning" Shannon, and that the discomfort was the direct results of eating all that junk food Maida had purchased with her bribe money. Even funnier was that Darden and I believed we had the upper hand in our children's social lives. Ha!

I must have been laughing aloud all of five minutes before Racina disturbed me with, "Mama, what'cha laughing at?"

"Oh, nothing important, child." That was a laconic reply, I know, but I neither forgave nor forgot so easily any more. I drifted right back into a yesteryear trance.

Racina wasn't really as motherly as she fronted to our nosy neighbors. Her hips rolled from side to side as her heels clicked on the cement walk from her car to the front porch. She knew she was pretty, after all, she had won the city's beauty contest that other year while still in high school. She also knew that had she not obeyed the insistance of her father and sister Maida, to stand and sit erect at all times, she might not have this posture so erect. But she was not about to admit that to anyone, hardly even to herself. She was so vain.

I decided to go in and take a quick nap. For whatever reason I felt tired. Maybe the middle-of-the-fall rays from the sun were warmer than I thought. About an hour later, I was crying out loud, pacing from my bedroom down and back up the narrow hall, and wringing my hands with every step I took.

Racina saw me and asked what was wrong.

"Nothing," I managed through my sobs, as I continued up and down the hall, believing now that Racina even resented my having a good cry, which was doing something that was *totally* of myself for that moment.

Racina said nothing more, then, but I knew she was watching me. I would cry for a little while, get quiet, cry fitfully for a few minutes, then get quiet again. I guess I went on like that for about thirty-five minutes before I sat in my gold chair, now moved from its spot in the living room and into my bedroom. I leaned my head backwards. When I finally closed my eyes, everything about Darden's death flooded my brain.

"Daddy didn't want me to know. He tried not to let me know, but the doctor said something was very wrong." These thoughts again made me aware that Darden's death had been both painful and swift. I began babbling the conversation in three voices: mine, Pectola's, and Darden's.

"He could barely hobble from the bedroom to the kitchen. He asked me to call for an ambulance because he wanted to go to the hospital. He had no strength to yell to me from the bedroom." Darden was seriously ill, and I wondered how I could have missed seeing signs of an illness. I was seriously frightened.

I tried tracing our lives from a few years back hoping I'd recognize some minute change in our daily routines. Darden's appetite for food had not diminished that I could recall. But about a year earlier, he had started drinking beer again, and I asked him about it.

"I have a lot of gas these days, and the beer provides the quickest way to expel it," Darden answered.

I thought at that time that Darden was providing an excuse to take up drinking again. I paid attention to his behavior for some time thereafter and found no further reason to discuss the beer thing again. Darden had stopped going for his daily walks at about the same time he started with the beer. He offered a reasonable excuse for that too.

"It just isn't safe walking along the Main Street Mall Corridor any more. Practically every day there is a mugging in broad daylight."

Of course I accepted Darden's words after viewing both television and newspaper reports about the increase in crime in our town.

Darden had kept secret the real reason for the changes taking place in his usual routines; he was seriously ill. After Darden was admitted to the hospital, it was his doctor who told me about Darden's terminal illness—cancer—and that he had perhaps less than six months to live. No, I didn't take that news well, not so much because of Darden's illness, but because Darden had kept the secret for over a year.

I didn't think that forgiving Darden was going to be easy. I was upset because he had not allowed me into his sickness. "…, in sickness and in health…," had been our vow to each other that beautiful day in July nearing seventy years ago.

On the third day of taking a taxi to visit Darden in the hospital, I was two hours earlier than on previous days. Darden took notice of the early arrival and greeted me warmly.

"Hi, Leanna, you're early today. I thought maybe you'd ask Pectola to be your driver to come to visit me. Did she drive you?"

"Never you mind about Pecky. Hi, yourself. Darden, you've got a bunch of explaining to do." I began to pace the floor in a path around the foot of his bed as I vented my rehearsed speech. "Darden, you've got to know that I'm feeling very hurt that you, for whatever reason, have kept your sickness from me. Pray tell, Darden, just what was or is your reason? My God, man, I'm your wife! How could you do this to me?" The volume of my voice had elevated to twice its normalcy.

"I didn't know how you were gonna react, Leanna. I just didn't know how to tell you."

"You got a mouth, don't you? Or did you maybe think writing me a note would say it better? I never got your note either. So what happened to it?"

"Leanna, you sound angry. Are you angry with me?"

I stopped pacing and faced him squarely. "Now, just what do you think? Here I've been married to you for over sixty years. And I thought, after that near breakup in the early years of our marriage, when we sincerely vowed our undying love to each other again, that we finally had a very stable relationship. But, no, I had to learn from your doctor that you've been sick for over a year, and that there is no more help left that they can give you. Darden, how could you do such a thing? How could you?"

"That's not how it was, Leanna. That's not how it was at all." At that very moment Darden was hit with a pain so severe that it jerked his head backward and his knees up to his chest.

My eyes stretched open wide enough for my eyeballs to spill out. I couldn't begin to understand why I had not seen such a thing happen to Darden before now. Moments later, in a mellowed tone, I spoke softly to him, "Darden, I know you remember that our wedding vows included the words, '…in sickness and in health….' I know you do. Well, I feel that you've robbed me of my privilege and my right to nurture you in your hour of sickness."

He recovered from that pain and said, "I wasn't trying to shut you out of my life, Leanna. I honestly didn't know how to tell you that I was not well. I'm sorry I've hurt you; I never meant to hurt you, ever again."

Apparently the stress of my visit was taking its toll on him as he was again writhing in pain. I stepped closer to the bedside, and whispered, "I believe you, Darden, and I forgive you. Uh, your doctor just stuck his head in the door. I'll let him get on with his job. I'll see you tomorrow, maybe early." I kissed him on the forehead then left his side to allow the doctor and nurse to comfort him in whatever was their manner.

I made a telephone call to Pectola and asked her to come over when she wasn't busy. When she arrived, I wasted no time in telling her that Darden was in the hospital. She didn't give me time to ask her to drive me to the hospital. Instead, she blurted out, "I'll be here to drive you to the hospital or any place any time of day you wish to go. Now, talk to me, girlfriend, I sense some anger. What else can you tell me?"

I quickly got on with my story. "After admitting Darden into the hospital four days ago, his doctor told me that my husband had known for over a year that he was seriously ill. I was so angry with Darden that I felt like striking him."

"So, tell me, had you noticed any changes in Darden during the past year?"

"Only that he had lost a little weight for one thing. He started drinking beer again, but his explanation of that was acceptable."

Pectola had always been a wonderful and true friend, and she was still into hearing, then leaking any bit of gossip that was available. Her words at that time could not be construed as searching for gossip.

Anyway, nowadays our gossip had to be about the younger generation because most of our peers were either deceased or they had moved away to be wherever one or more of their offspring lived who could share in the caring for them. And those who still lived in Graybar were too entrenched in their hypochondriases to be interesting or even mildly entertaining. Pecky and I considered ourselves as still being with it, functioning as did the younger crowds.

We sorely missed our friend, Nola Mae, who had died a year earlier from complications due to a stroke. Now, when Pecky and I got together, we usually repeated some remark that Nola Mae would have prefaced our 'girly' meetings with, and that remark would set the tone for our present meeting. That would not be happening on this particular day.

On the next day, when Pecky arrived to drive me to the hospital, she sensed a macabre moment. She cordially greeted me and decided to let me open up a conversation.

"Hi, Pecky. Come on in for a moment. I'm a little low today, and I want to tell you all about it."

"Surely, Leanna. Do tell, what's up?"

"Well, first, what I haven't told you is exactly why Darden is in the hospital. Yes, he's been ill for some time, and he did a superb job of keeping me in the dark. The doctor told me that Darden has cancer. And he never said a word about it to me." My eyes teared and I blinked rapidly to stop any overflow of water.

"Le, are you angry with Darden because he is ill?"

"Yes, but not because he is ill. I'm angry because Darden has long known that he maybe had only six months to live. The cancer has spread throughout his body. I had it out with him about it, yesterday. He said he had not meant to hurt me, ever again. He did hurt me, but I have forgiven him. I guess I'm more sad now than still angry with him."

"Girl friend, I wish I could offer you something to ease your discomfort."

"Oh, just having you here to listen lifts a heavy burden from my heart. I'm so glad I still have you for a friend."

Okay, right here, let me just tell you how Pectola had earned my friendship many years ago. Pectola not only heard what one had to say, but she listened to what one was saying with their words before she reacted in any manner. That had intrigued me. Most people never learn to do that: hear, and listen.

Pectola told me sometime ago, that most of the people who knew my family, believed true love existed equally between myself and Darden. Pecky almost convinced me that she believed she could write a three-hundred page book just about Darden's and my relationship with each other. She knew that the six or seven years so very long ago, when Darden was full of the devil's rage, had long been forgotten, and long been forgiven.

I felt a great sigh of relief after telling Pectola the full truth. We left for the hospital and a visit with Darden.

The first words Darden spoke to Pectola were, "Thank you, Pecky, for being Leanna's friend."

"I wouldn't be anything else. She's so adorable. In fact, the two of you have been my lifeline since Thurston passed away, how could I not reciprocate? I love you both."

It was only a few days more that Darden was confined in the hospital. Once he was home, I reiterated to him that I forgave him for his lack of courtesy in letting me know of his illness.

And so the two of us, Darden and myself, continued on with our lives knowing there would be some changes. A major change was Darden's acceptance of Pecky's offer to be our chauffeur for whatever the occasion, as he felt I was beyond a sensible age to try to learn to drive. And so, there would be no need to disturb the work schedules of our children or grandchildren who lived here in town. Darden came with me to the grocery stores and helped shorten the time necessary for making purchases.

Darden enjoyed lots of days of feeling well enough to tackle tasks similar to ones he had done before he became so ill. Some of the tasks were rather involved. One in particular was replacing the kitchen floor tiles, something he had planned as a surprise only a day before he was hospitalized. On any day he was feeling very well, he was anxious to get started on his surprise job. He hoped to get me occupied elsewhere in the house by asking me to mend several pieces of his clothing on my sewing machine. I agreed and retired to my sewing room.

I was nearly finished with the sewing when I heard Darden's labored breathing. I rushed from the sewing room toward the sounds and dicovered Darden replacing the kitchen floor tiles. I held fast to my scold words, and instead knelt down beside him and gave him my support. That he would attempt such a thing was idiotic, but I stayed calm about it once I realized the job was more than half over. It took the two of us half an hour longer and the job was completed. Darden understood that the help I offered him with things he couldn't quite complete was not pity, but just his loving wife being his wife.

From time to time I would ask Darden how he was feeling at a given moment, only out of love, not pity. And he would answer truthfully because he realized just how much it meant for me to be there for him.

The day soon came that the two of us looked back at the last milestones we had chanced, and we enjoyed a healthy laugh together. Darden no longer dwelled on his stupidity, and I no longer dwelled on my anger. Once more our lives were in sync as had long been our marital forte.

Racina must have overheard my conversation in the three voices. She would have entered my room, maybe to join in the conversation, but changed her mind when she heard me ask, then answer, "Is Daddy sick? Is he?" "Oh no, nothing ever bothers him. He's just trying to tease me."

She stood for a long while listening just outside my door. She was showing real concern, now.

My conversation continued, "But when I turned around and saw that face—his forehead furrowed, his eye sockets stretched wide open—that instant I knew that he was depending on my help. I did call for an ambulance. And I called Racina, Neva, and Braxton, and left messages for them at work to meet me at County Regional Hospital, now!

"There's no excuse for him not telling me before now that he didn't feel well. Heck, yeah, sometimes I get a twinge or two in my lower back when I try to get up in the mornings. I suspect all old people do. That's nothing to be ashamed of. In fact, because you're old is a good reason for telling somebody that all is not well with you.

"I wish Daddy had told me that he had been to a doctor and the doctor had told him he had cancer. Maybe I didn't know what to do about it. Maybe I would have felt sorry for him. I just won't ever get the chance to know, now." Momentary pseudo-anger disallowed me the exactness of those sickness details. I had forgiven Darden, but never could forget that he had excluded me from most of the days of his illness.

"And after all these years living with this man, he didn't trust me enough to let me in on his most secret of all secrets—that he had cancer! The darn doctor had to tell me that he had cancer, not one, but two kinds, and the cancer had spread throughout his body. He said he marvelled at Darden's ability to hide the effects of the debilitating and torturous disease, especially after he told him he had about six months to live.

"Three months later we buried my Darden." Then after a long pause, "I guess I'll forgive him. Oh, I do forgive him. How could I not? I still love him." Those were the exact words that I spoke to Pectola, my longtime friend.

"Pectola, you've always understood us. You knew what I was going through with that man. You've helped me to understand Darden's behavior more than a few times. You were the friend on the outside looking in." That reference was to Darden's wild days those six or seven years so very long ago.

Racina only left her post outside my bedroom door when she heard me snoring. Sleep had come; my pain was eased.

CHAPTER 8

▼

THE NEST IS EMPTY

There was a long spell of time when I wished my children would hurry up and get grown, and move out on their own. I know now that I harbored much guilt during that time, and that it was my two closest friends, Pectola and Nola Mae, who helped me through such guilt trips. It was when all of the children were on their own that my friends told me that they had read books by leading American psychologists that spoke of the Empty Nest Syndrome.

It was no wonder that I always seemed tired, physically, mentally, but never morally. No, I wouldn't sacrifice my faith for anyone, including my children. In fact, I and my children were faithful to God and worshipped at the small Methodist church located just two blocks from our home. Thankfully, none of the children ever tried to pull the "stomachache" trick just to stay home and miss a worship service.

Physically, I was tired from my years of cooking, cleaning, washing, ironing, and having babies. I was thankful for the help that Darden afforded me by buying our groceries weekly, and doing all of the necessary chores until I was on my feet again after the introduction of a new mouth.

I was almost beside myself with exhilaration when our youngest, Neva, was married. Yep, it meant nothing less than our household would be empty of children. Now, don't misunderstand me, I dearly loved each and every one of our children, but it was time to think of moving on to other things for myself and Darden. Mostly myself, that is, because I felt I had fully earned the right to something solely for me, no one else.

I began my newfound joy by spending much of the leftover weekly salary on clothing for myself. It wasn't long before my friends were considering me a fashion-plate.

I had always been well-dressed, but I had sewn all of my own clothing, and most of the clothing for our children. The nest is empty now, and I don't have to sew my own anymore.

When I could, I would travel to Cayuga to visit with my remaining siblings. My two older brothers, you remember that their jobs transferred them to New York, had died. My favorite brother, Mitchell, was not well. He was suffering from cancer now. Breast cancer. Yep, breast cancer.

Zeena, the stalwart member of the family, still opened her doors to the visiting family. A hilarious time would be had, when only moments after one's arrival, the word would be out, and Zeena's home soon would be swarming with family and close friends. Well into the night, we would talk, almost as if it had been years upon years since one had seen the other, when it might only have been just six months earlier.

I am going to admit something right now. Although I truly enjoyed my visits with my family, deep in my subconscious, I held a resentment of my siblings' personalities. I saw them as free-spirited, unlike myself so socially shy, except when in church. As a small child, I was not learned enough to think for myself about my clothes, my playtime, or my playmates. As a teenager, I allowed my brother, Mitchell, to persuade me to be selective in choosing my friends. Mitchell had said that because I was so beautiful, yes he did say that, many would think me naive and so try to take advantage. As Darden's wife, I allowed him to control every aspect of my life—how many children we would have, where we would live, and how we would interact socially. The only thing solely mine was my religious belief. And though I stood steadfast in my faith, no one ever ventured calling me a religious fanatic.

So you see, although I was fully grown, a mother several times over, and the maternal glue of my own household, with the nest now empty, I knew I had not yet realized freedom. And I wanted to be free, as free as I witnessed my sisters and brothers. I vowed that I must know freedom. I must stand tall. Make decisions by myself, for myself, about myself, and do as I pleased.

Since being bitten by the "go" bug, I was forever ready to do just that—go. You bet I did, I kept a valise always packed. I traveled by bus, by train, and yes that too, by airplane, after I finally worked up the nerve.

When I was ready to make my first airplane trip, Darden tried to be funny. He teased, "Have you got your diapers handy?"

"Oh, you. I don't need any diapers, I'm no baby. At least I'm willing to try flying, you won't even do that!" To those words, I spun around on my toes, and with a sway in my hips, sashayed down the hallway to our bedroom, laughing all the way.

Racina was almost seventeen by the time Darden had saved up enough money to purchase the first car for our family. No one knew that, secretly, he had been taking driving lessons in preparation for owning his first car, and to be the one to drive that car off the new car sales parking lot himself.

And so after one year, Racina and Neva got to drive the car. Each had taken driving lessons as part of their high school curriculum and earned "A" grades. Darden was confident he would still have a car after they had driven it. They did so well that he allowed them to drive me for a visit with the children who had moved far away to northern states. We made the trip safely and without incident.

Oh, yes, let me tell you about a special trip I made. I call it a special trip because it was a cruise. You heard me right, a cruise. I was invited to take a trip on a cruise ship with my daughter and granddaughter. To everyone's surprise, and maybe to my own surprise at that time, yes, I accepted. Now, you remember, I'd always been sorely afraid of waterways. Yet, I held to the decision, because it was *my* decision. *My decision!*

All of the family was shocked, Darden included, but he had nothing negative to say. They all believed I would back out of the agreement when the time slot narrowed to a few days before sailing time.

When the time to sail got close, Darden couldn't resist teasing me.

"Honey, are you sure you have enough diapers, you know, the throw-away kind? You won't have time to be washing any soiled cotton ones."

"Oh, you just shut up. I'm going on this cruise, and leaving you sitting in that old chair. So, there!"

"Don't get too smart for your britches, now. I didn't give you permission to go." He continued his teasing.

"Say what? You didn't give me permission to go? Ha! You must think you're my daddy."

"I don't *think* it, I *know* it. I'm your *Sugar Daddy.*"

All the family members who had come to see us off just rolled and bellowed with laughter. I continued to laugh, for weeks and weeks, at least, every time I remembered that remark that had come out of Darden's mouth.

Whew! Gosh! Why am I shivering so? I don't know when I've felt so cold. "Oh my gosh, why did I say I would go out on some ocean cruise? I never liked the river, and I could see its shores. If I go out on some ocean, I won't be able to see any shore from where we'll be sailing." I'd better sit down, if I'm going to be crying tears like this.

Just as suddenly as I started crying, I stopped, wiped my eyes and smiled. I began remembering the hilarious time aboard ship that my daughter Maida, granddaughter Grace, and I had in the room that had a bath facility so tiny, each one of us had to fight off the wet shower curtain that clung to our bodies like wet tee shirts the entire time we were showering. And, when we entered the cubby-hole sized room which had to have been designed for a single occupancy instead of three, just the size of it alone brought on laughter so hard, that each one of us tried to beat out the other to the toilet before we peed our pants. Yep, we, all three, lost, every night! Our room attendant must have thought that the three of us had weak bladders, or we only had two pairs of panties apiece. The attendant saw three different sizes of panties hanging up to dry each morning that he entered the room to do his cleaning.

But, guess what? Not once during those seven days aboard that ship did I have fear of the water. And the ship heaved for one *full* day while it battled the choppy waves of the open sea. Those in charge of entertainment aboard the ship sure did keep us busy. I was vying for prizes for being the oldest grandmother aboard ship, as well as for having the most children, most grandchildren, and most great-grandchildren. *And I won!*

I think I forgot to tell you early on, that the cruise trip was a graduation gift for my granddaughter, and a birthday gift for me. Yep, I was celebrating my eighty-second birthday out there on the Atlantic Ocean, being especially catered to. At dinner time, the waiters for our table delivered to me a special-made birthday cake. Each waiter carried a lighted candle. They asked that the room lights be dimmed. Then everyone sang happy birthday to me and shared equivalent birthday cakes.

At each port call, I relied on some energy reserve I must have stored away, because I was ready, willing and able to venture to the on-shore shops. I even went on sightseeing bus tours that were offered to the passengers. I was so excited. For quite a few years more, that excitement hung with me. I guess my friends, and acquaintances, got tired of hearing me say, "We just had a grand time."

When we returned home from the trip, I had gift prizes for each of my children, each grandchild, and each great-grandchild. I traveled for years, first here, then there, and almost everywhere there was a relative. I slowed when Darden showed signs of physical stress.

CHAPTER 9

▼

THE SWELTON
CHILDREN

Thinking back, I have been dancing to the tunes of drummers not my own for all of my life. And now that I'm a widow, I feel the need to be free to dance only to my own drummer. I don't think my children have enough of an understanding, or maybe they just refuse to understand, that freedom is due me. And due me, *now!*

I keep using up my sane time flashing back to when my children were children. I call it my "sane" time, for I am aware that I am no longer remembering most of the details of each one's yesteryear. But, I continue to strive to stay in touch with reality for as long as I possibly can. That's why now, I'm looking backwards to find a spark of something that will clue me in on why my children are spending so much time with me lately. I'm not finding any sparks.

"Perhaps my children think that I am so lost since Darden's death that I will wander helplessly about and end up someplace in a stupor." Now, that's a scary thought.

I can tell you this. All eight of the children made up a well-knit family. And that was acknowledged by the people in our community who, looking in from the outside, made comments about how devoted the children were to Darden and myself. But of course, the outside community was never witness to verbal abuse that Darden sometimes heaped upon me which prompted our children to visibly stalk him, as if ready to pounce upon him and attempt some physical harm. Of course, *no* situation ever progressed to that point.

I do remember the time that Darden so crowded me into a corner and three of our first four children thought they saw him strike me. Well! Edril raced from the room and quickly returned carrying his father's hammer. When Larson and Maida saw this, they scampered from the room and returned with "weapons"—Larson's was part of a broken yardstick, and Maida's was a dirty dust cloth. Their scampering noise attracted Darden's attention, causing him to abort whatever were his intentions. He abruptly left the room. The confrontation was over.

I can say with certainty that although the children never saw Darden drink any alcoholic beverages, they grew to recognize the telltale signs—his harsh words directed to me, and his unsteadiness afoot almost always well after dark. Darden's biting words to me usually made no sense to the children, but once they heard his soured tone, one or more of them would quietly become visible to him so as to stifle any further abuse to me. I thought it quite odd, but Darden never vented his alcohol-powered hostility on the children. Instead, it seemed that the sight of one of them cuffed and cloaked the demon within him, shutting it off from further exposure to anyone.

The "foolishness," the label the children used for Darden's behavior, lasted some six or seven years before it disappeared, and Darden's and my relationship returned to the normalcy and closeness that the children had known in their earliest years. I'm sure the children, overall, learned a lesson—one person cannot change another person's character; instead, that person changes his character of his own volition.

Those several communities in Graybar, neighborhood, church, school, and peer groups, that had witnessed the birth of most and the rearing of all of our children saw something good in all of them. At one time, only the young peer group community rumbled false negatives about my children. Their rumbles were fueled mostly by jealousy, a jealousy about the kind of parental love they saw in our family and wished was a part of their own. There was little that the communities in Graybar did not know about Darden Swelton's Family.

Let me tell you what I remember about the childhood of each of my children, without looking at a photo album.

Edril is the oldest of our sons. He was always so quiet, something almost unheard of in any small child. I don't think that I considered him "slow;" instead, his quietness meant he was busy mentally examining the "how come" and the "what for" of physical objects caught in his sight. Whenever he could, with his younger brother Larson's help, Edril would proceed to explore or examine those objects. No, Larson was not along simply to give Edril eyesight support.

"Hey, L.D., gimme that small wrench over there." L.D. was how Edril shortened Larson David.

Larson chimed back, "Ya mean this'n?"

"Yeah, tha'sit. Now you stand over here so you won't be hit if this thing comes off in the air."

"Well," Larson would say, pointing to a mound of debris, "can'tcha put one of them rags over it before you turn it?"

"If'n I did that, then I couldn't see what I'm doing. I need to see what I'm doing, you know."

"Eder, wha'cha gonna make when you're done?" Larson was all of nine years old before he could say Edril's name correctly.

"I'm not sure. If the thing comes away like I think it oughta, I'll make us a shoe-wide scooter."

"You don't know how no scooter is made. You don't, do you?"

"I got me a pretty good idee. And an idee is all I need, little brother."

Edril pursued his natural curiosity and became a "mechanical engineer," the jack-of-all-trades kind, as an adult. He made a darn good living at it, too. In fact, his services were in such demand that he forfeited earning a college degree after one and a half years and got on with living his adulthood doing what he loved best—breaking apart and rebuilding whatever.

Larson, as a child, would not always obey our wishes, yet he was not intending to be disrespectful the way I saw him. He was insistent that his male peers understand his rule if ever they pestered his little sister Maida. That part of his behavior mimicked my relationship with my brother Mitchell, except I was the older of us two.

In school, if a boy had designs on Maida and maybe dipped her long hair braids into the inkwell of the desk behind her own, his behavior could certainly bring on a fist duel with her brother Larson. Sometimes a boy might throw small stones at Maida because she rejected his attention. That behavior was a definite no-no and earned the boy a fist duel with Larson. A time or two, even though the offender may have left the area of his offense and reached the safety of his own home, Larson was bold enough to follow him and call him out for a fist duel, all to appease his sister's honor. I also have to clue you that whether his duels were with big or bigger bullies, Larson took total charge.

Larson's life interest lay in the physical sciences, especially after his preliminary testing for mandatory military service revealed a bent toward such. He completed all of three college years before he was smitten with love for this one girl. He proposed, was accepted, and married the girl of his dreams. They started a family before Larson found steady work, which proved to be disastrous for them. Darden helped them financially when he witnessed the couple's dire need. It was not enough to hold the marriage together. The mother won custody of their child, and Larson promised her regular child support.

Before long, Larson got word of "good paying jobs" opening in the steel mills of Pennyslvania. He hastened to be one of the lucky ones to be hired. He did well financially, and so faithfully supported his son. He didn't remarry the mother of his son, but he did marry once more.

Maida was the timid one of our children. Larson had sensed it by the time Maida was five, and took it upon himself to look after her safety. Maybe his being of stocky build compared to Edril's lean frame was how he first got the idea that he was tough and should be Maida's protector.

Maida had encounter after encounter with boys who always used the wrong tactics to attract her attention. When she reached tenth grade, she was well schooled in handling her own defense. She did like the attention most of the boys paid her, except for Roland who sat directly behind her in class. He liked to poke his feet through the opening between the back and bottom of her desk chair and soil her clothes. That would make her fighting mad.

"Roland," Maida turned and said to him, "don't put your feet on my clean clothes."

He made no audible reply, just grinned deceptively.

Maida returned her attention to the math problem she was trying to solve when she felt her skirt move again. She turned in her seat and spoke again.

"I told you, Roland, don't put your feet on my clean clothes."

"Oh, did I do that?"

"You're the only one sitting behind me," she replied, struggling to remain polite. Her eyes, she thought, would convey her real message.

Her eyes were not menacing enough, for it was a moment later that she felt her skirt move. This time Maida leaped from her seat, turned around and faced Roland squarely. She promised, "You touch anything of mine once more and you'll be sorry!"

"Oh, you gonna tell your big brother on me?"

"I wouldn't try me if I were you. I might just have something for you of my own." Maida sat down.

Everyone in the class except the teacher heard Maida, or so Roland thought, making it too late for him to back down in any way. He hesitated just long enough for Maida to think she had scared him, then he pulled her hair and dragged his foot on her skirt through the seat opening.

Without further words, Maida stood up and slammed her fist into Roland's face, which startled him into throwing up his hands to protect himself. The teacher heard and saw the scuffle between the two and demanded they come to her desk immediately.

Absolutely no one knew that Maida would or could pack such a wallop. In truth, neither did she. Anyway Maida and Roland were escorted to the principal's office. Roland received an off-campus suspension of one day for abusing a female schoolmate. Maida was harshly scolded for fighting on school grounds.

Maida continued her schooling and was the first of the children to finish college. You should also know that all the while she attended college she operated her own sewing business. Her degree, earned in business administration, helped her to get immediate employment in private industry. She fazed out her sewing contracts. Two years later she married and moved away to West Virginia.

Back then, I was aware that all of Maida's accomplishments did not endear her to her sisters. Instead, their resentment and jealousy towards her led them to push her outside the family circle, beginning when the girls were mere teenagers. The first "excuse" voiced for their behavior was, "She knows so darn much." Later, the excuse, "You live so far away," was used when they didn't tell her about happenings within the family circle.

Maida's peers and friends had warned her that her siblings had a miffed attitude about her. They told her they knew of family gatherngs where all were in attendance except for her. Maida stood strongly in total denial for years, "Certainly my family would not do that to me." I believe that when Darden died, Maida found reason to finally come out of denial about her sibling's treatment of her.

All but two of the children had arrived for the occasion of their father's funeral, and had gathered in one room. During a conversation, one spoke something that made the others laugh heartily. That is, all but Maida, who had not understood what had been said. "What are you laughing at? What could be so funny?"

"Nothing," came the chortled reply.

"That kind of laughter is started up by something. Come on, what were you laughing at?"

"Nothing," was again the concerted reply.

Maida's outcry, "If you don't want me to know what's going on, fine. I can take a hint."

The remark only prompted the siblings to laugh harder. Maida was visibly shaken by their insult; she left the room and the house. She returned the next day for a short visit alone with me. I'm about certain that it took Maida two years before she could exhibit solid composure when in the presence of the rest of the children.

I'm admitting, now, that at the time of this type of discord, I honestly thought it was nothing more than some teasing going on, and I felt that the teasing could soften the seriousness of the occasion for all of them being at the house.

Braxton, our youngest son, was himself the devil's imp. No, I don't mean he was evil. He simply thought his tricks were harmless and funny. He used me as a testing ground for his tricks, and when I didn't thwack him about any one trick, he felt free to try that trick on someone else.

From the time Braxton was walking well, he exhibited a condition called somnambulism. We realized that he blamed us, his parents, for putting this "curse" on him. For a long while, only his best buddies knew about the condition, and they had found out when he spent nights in their homes at slumber parties. Yep, boys talk also, so that bit of trivia got leaked to the church community, then on to the school community, and most certainly elsewhere. From this humiliation, Braxton created an escape route—harmless pranks which covered his "curse" well. He did outgrow the condition before he was eighteen, but the pranks-personae were already entrenched.

One other thing I remember about Braxton is how close he was with his younger sisters than with his older brothers. I'm guessing that came about because he really couldn't gain a foothold of power with his brothers, while he held all the power with his sisters.

The onlooking Graybar communities had varying views of my younger girls. Cordice and Racina were viewed for most of their childhood like two peas in a pod—most always together. These two did not shun Neva. It was Neva who most times lived in her own world caring for her doll babies. When Neva tired of her "mothering" duties, she would join with Cordice and Racina, and the three played well together.

Occasionally, Cordice pulled cutesies on Racina by telling her little white lies. Now, if Racina acted on Cordice's words, she sometimes found herself in hot water with me.

"Racina, Mama said for you to put on your pink and white dress today."

"When did Mama tell you that?"

"When I was downstairs gettin' me a glass o' water. And she said you better mind me 'cause I'm older than you."

"Oh, Cordice, you lyin'. You know Mama ain't told you nothing." She was nearly finished with lacing her left shoe. "How come you lie like that?" They were at the great young ages of nine and seven.

"Okay. Don't believe me then. I don't care." She tossed her head up to the right, and licked her tongue out at Racina. "It ain't gonna be me gettin' no switchin' for not doing wha'cha been told to do."

Racina, my feisty child, was not really afraid of getting a whipping, but she just wasn't ready to have Cordice pull another "duh" on her and be laughing at her behind her back.

Perhaps an hour passed before Racina came to me. "Mama," she said, "Cordice told me you said I should put on my pink and white dress today."

"Oh. And you did what she said?" I stood looking at her over the rim of my glasses positioned low on my nose.

"Well, yessum, and that's how I got it dirty, too, I bleeved her."

"Now, Racina, you knew you were to wear that dress in the school play tonight. Now it's dirty. Go get me that bar of Octagon soap, take off the dress and bring them both back here. I'll try cleaning it in time for the play."

"Mama, I'm sorry. I ought'n bleeved Cordice. I know that now. I ain't gonna get no switchin' am I?"

"I'll deal with the two of you later." Many times, trust my words on this, I've heaved exasperated sighs about the antics those two often stumbled into. No, I didn't wear myself out trying to discipline them with a switch or any weapon. That would have clued them in that what they were doing was really getting my goat. I had to remain the parent. Racina, in her heart, was never terribly angry with Cordice for her fibs, even when acknowledging those fibs did lead to a switching.

I'm also remembering that no one in our Graybar communities ever spoke badly about any of our children. It is true that some of the Graybar communities had witnessed some adverse behaviors in our children, and I knew that time would eventually expose those behaviors. Darden and I were aware that once a child married, moved away and started his or her own family, the need to continue devotion to the parents took a back seat. We accepted what we knew the children felt— that they had a right to live their own lives.

Edril was the first of our children to move with his family back to the general area of Graybar, some seventy miles southeast. Edril had accepted a government contract and had agreed to their relocation bid. His first job was proving to be quite a task, but he was determined to have it completed by its posted due date.

He had promised to visit with us over that weekend and was en route to our home when the accident occurred. Edril trusted his old jalopy to Graybar and back almost under its own steering. The lesser traveled road that he chose to drive, crossed railroad tracks just past a curve in the road. He had not heard the train's whistle, *if it blew,* so he rounded the curve and was crossing the tracks when the car lurched, then stopped. He felt the ground rumbling under him and knew it was the train coming. He reached down and unfastened his seatbelt, but was too late for rolling out of and away from the car before the train hit the vehicle. By the time the ambulance got him to the hospital he had been pronounced dead.

I must have cried for all of three days it took for the other children to arrive for Edril's funeral. Though it had been all of those many years ago that Darrell had died, it felt like I was experiencing that kind of death all over again. I was again having thoughts that God was seeing me as less than his faithful servant. Even with Darden standing like a rock at my side, I did regress. Again, I turned to the church for comfort, and opted to read the Bible for longer periods of each day. On the day Edril was buried, it was as if Darden's hand turned into God's hand and he dried my tears.

I learned a lot about the less fortunate youth of our church and offered a helping hand. I volunteered to teach cooking to any of the youth who wanted to learn. About seven showed up the first day. When it was learned they got to eat the food they cooked, ten showed for the next few days. The church furnished everything. Darden raised no objections to what I was doing. He felt he understood the why when my nights again became restless.

Shannon's death followed Edril's death in only two years. She and her oldest daughter were driving to Graybar for a visit with us when they ran into a sudden rain downpour. There was no way of knowing how long it had been storming in that area, so Shannon did not know that flash flood warnings had been made. She had slowed her speed and knew she was driving safely under those weather conditions, but she was upon a wide water puddle before she realized the road had disappeared. She applied the breaks, but her car got swept up in the furious currents of the water puddle and was sucked under where a roadbed had once been. Panic overwhelmed them, so neither had time to escape the vehicle. Their bodies were still buckled in when the car came to rest on an embankment one and a half miles south of where it had gone under water. That road had become a river.

I'm just not good at holding up whenever I'm presented with stressful or traumatic information. The first question asked when I answered the telephone was, "Do you have a daughter named Shannon Swelton Bronne?" My answer was a reluctant, "Yes." I wanted to know to whom I was speaking, but he hurriedly got in a second question. "Ma'am, would Eunice Bronne Mason be your granddaughter?" Then, I hesitated an answer and asked of the speaker, "And, just who are you, and why are you asking me these questions?" He said who he was, then offered an apology for having to be the bearer of sad news.

Upon receiving the news, that my daughter and granddaughter had been drowned in a flash flood, my knees buckled and my legs gave way under me. This time, there was no person close by to abort my inevitable slump to the floor. My voice, also weakened by the news, was barely audible, and that's why it took me all of five minutes to summon help. A neighbor from across the street just happened by for a neighborly visit and heard my feeble cry for help. She did not know at that moment that I was home alone.

Unbelievable, but these deaths did not present the same depth of despair to me. Instead, I now knew that which was God's will was His will being done. Gratefully, I accepted Darden's hand which to me became God's hand again drying my tears.

In the beginning and shortly after Racina moved into my home, she was elated that the other children visited me often and offered her a helping hand. Larson and Neva had moved back to Graybar and were available for any emergencies that could arise. Braxton lived only a few miles away but in our home state. And though Cordice and Maida lived out of state, they made fairly frequent stopins. At first, all of my children included me in their frolicking about town, and that gave Racina moments to be by herself.

Not so long after Racina moved in, I also got the impression that my children believed I was rapidly reaching a "confused and lost" state. But, I wanted only to do what I wanted to do.

Perhaps it was but about four years after Darden died that the children began to slow their visits which left Racina the sole responsibility of looking after me. That is what Racina had said she intended to do when she moved in, but she never imagined that her siblings would leave her to do just that.

Tragedy plagued this Swelton family once more. Larson, for whatever reason, had become a heavy drinker of alcohol. He was away from his home and on one of his drinking sprees when he ventured into the Stay-Low Bar and Grill where he encountered a man who was accusing him of insulting his wife. Larson let the liquor do his talking when he told the man, "That's right. Kick a man when he's down. Ha, ha. But you're right. I told her she was u-g-l-y, and she is. Ha, ha, ha."

Larson was pummeled to the floor by the man, who got some help from two other men in the bar. By the time they stopped beating him, his head was a bloody mess. The bartender called for the police and an ambulance. The police arrived but learned nothing about the attackers who had fled the scene, except that they had mentioned they were passing through town. The police took Larson to the hospital where he lost his fight for survival two days later. No one knew his attackers so no one was ever charged with his murder.

The loss of Larson dealt me a crushing blow. Without Darden at my side to help me absorb the senseless devastation, I was hearing my head music louder and louder. I sometimes violently shook my head trying to shut down the music. One day I even said aloud, "That noise is annoying me now!"

And so, for longer hours daily, I would sit and read my Bible. I seemed to have slipped a bit in my thoughts about God's intent for all of his children, me included. I needed to shore up the weakened area. I got transported to church every Sunday, by one or the other of my children who lived in town, but I wasn't as aware of the meanings in the minister's messages.

I'm not saying this for sure, but just maybe, I'm not quite as sharp as I thought I was just a few days ago, or perhaps I should say, a few weeks ago. I don't want to confuse myself. When I don't want to solo-think, I get my Bible and begin to read. That way, I force myself to focus on the intentions of someone else.

Right here, I must admit that my children have always respected my time set aside for Bible reading. And the way I see things, my Bible reading time is the *only* time they give me sincere respect. For that I'm very appreciative, for I *need* to get more in touch with God and learn what he has in store for me for the rest of my life.

I also have a second fascination, reading about Greek culture. I'm not sure, but I believe that Shannon was in seventh grade, and was studying Civilization, or maybe it was called Civics then. Anyway, she came home one day, very excited about Gods. It seemed that in the Greek culture, there was more than one God, and these Gods appeared in human form. Well, my own schooling had reached no higher than sixth grade with boundaries no wider than the shores of the United States. I guess I've always had a curious mind, so I got real curious. The more Shannon came home with her excitable words on Greek culture, the more curious I became. My imagination conjured up such weird scenarios about that culture that I decided to visit our public library and read about it for myself.

Back then, I got good enough to challenge Darden on his knowledge of Greek mythology, to the point that I'm sure he found a way to read up on it at the library just to best me. For many nights and many years longer, we had super conversations with our children, our grands, friends, church youth, and even some of the neighborhood busybodies. It came to pass, though, that after Darden died, only one young neighbor and I had such talks. The church youth with whom I had become esteemed continued to stop in and we enjoyed pleasant visits mostly just talking trivia. Years ago, these youth had voiced their adoration because I had taught them cooking and sewing skills when no one else cared about them. "Mrs. Swelton, you were our inspiration to go forth and achieve our own greatness."

Our baby girl, Neva, had kept a secret from us for over twelve years. She thought telling us that she had leukemia, an incurable disease, would simply be too much for us to handle, especially following the deaths of her siblings. Neva gave up her fight against leukemia one year after the murder of Larson.

The tunes in my head are overlapping now. Sometimes I think I hear three or four at the same time. That's when I sit for a few minutes, read from my Bible, then walk out onto the front porch and pause by the center support pole and hum a tune. I sit and rock with my eyes closed only for a few moments, then reenter the house and sit in my tattered gold chair and cry.

It wasn't long after Neva's death that the Graybar communities began a cynical vigil of my children, trying to determine the sincerity of the attention each paid to me. "Her children have been fronting devotion all these years," some said. Some others said, "By and by there's gonna be some trouble in that camp. Sibling rivalry is bound to get fierce."

The company Maida worked for had moved her family quite a distance away, and given her unpredictable work schedules—three months each in four different states with time off for traveling, and maybe for sandwiching in mini-vacations with her family. Any time she could spare was when she visited with me.

Braxton became steadfastly occupied either with his job or his family to the point that he had next to no time for visiting with me. Everybody knew that I had never entertained anything negative with my daughters-in-law, but of late, each daughter-in-law maintained stiff, almost hostile, formalities when in my presence. I'm guessing that because I wasn't always at the same time-spot in memory with everyone, the infrequent lucidity didn't allow me the luxury of poignant rebuttals to any unpleasant situations with the daughters-in-law. "Don't you think that turned into a blessing for me?"

By the time I was ninety-two, the Graybar communities began witnessing the turnabout frequency of visitations by my children and all of their families. My neighborhood community believed that such trafficking would be devastating to me.

CHAPTER 10

▼

"MS. LEANNA"

Surely, you've heard the expression, "It's a small world." I have and I'm older than you, so I know you have too.

Just tell me, what are the odds of grandchildren of the children who were once inseparable playmates moving into the same community that is miles upon miles away from the area of first existence and getting to know one another well enough to realize they have a *lot* in common? Now, that is when one might hear, or say, the expression, "It's a small world, after all."

I believe that I was already past my eighty-first birthday when Dee revealed she was the grandchild of my childhood playmate Amelia Poussant. Amelia and I had almost grown up together in Cayuga where we were born, and we had been neighbors in the same block, and had taken turns being the first to knock on the other one's door seeking a playmate on every fair day. Of course, all of this took place before a mandatory separation lasting about six years took effect in my family's home. Amelia and I were all of seven years old at the onset of that separation. The separation did not undo, for me and Amelia, the great friendship that had begun when we were mere babies.

Let me tell you about Dee so you will be on the same page as me. I like saying things like that as it makes me feel kinda special. Anyway, Dee was visiting one day, oops, I'm the one off page, already, so I'll start up again.

Dee Granger was the daughter of Geraldine Armond Granger who was the daughter of Amelia Poussant Armond. Geraldine was only nineteen when she married Harold Granger and moved away from Cayuga. Dee was an only child of an only child, and got to visit her widowed grandmother Amelia in Cayuga for the whole of every summer. "Those were such happy times," Dee said, "when age difference nor family relationship stymied our great friendship."

Dee told me that her "Nana Armond" flabbergasted her with tales of her young years growing up in Cayuga. Those tales were mostly about myself and her grandmother. "We, too, played hopscotch, jackrocks, Stickball, jump rope, and 'house' where the girls did all of the cooking and the boys went off to their jobs," Dee said her grandmother repeated those same words to her so often that she conjured up pictures of what "Leanna" must have looked like, especially since it was "Leanna" who always seemed to win their play games. Dee told me that her grandmother repeatedly said, "They were the best years of my life. We played so well together, all of us. We did get separated from Leanna about the time we were seven years old, but by the time Leanna was returned home, about age twelve or thirteen, my parents had moved to a neighborhood across town. Because our families had no telephones, motor vehicles, or horses with buggies, it was difficult for us to be in frequent touch. We remained friends by posting real notes to each other explaining all of what each one was doing in the other's absence.

Just out of college and twenty-one years old, Dee Granger married Marshall Norton, her college sweetheart, and they began their married life in Graybar, Marshall's home town. Dee had met Marshall, and my granddaughter, Clarice Bailey, in college and they had become best friends. Often, Dee visited Graybar as the weekend guest of Clarice who already knew Marshall Norton from her church.

Chance conversations that Dee and Marshall had with Clarice about their families eventually led Dee to realize that her grandmother, Amelia Poussant Armond, and Clarice's grandmother, me—Leanna Mallard Swelton, had been those special childhood friends back there in Cayuga, Tennessee.

Mentally armed with that kind of connection, that was all the reason Dee needed to get to know me and Darden better. We were quite comfortable with Dee and Marshall frequently visiting with us.

We talked about everything under the sun, which most times included some input about Greek mythology. You see, Darden was as fascinated with Greek mythology as I, and he loved challenging their young minds to help him with his interpretation of the "religion" of a yesteryear.

"Well, if the Greeks worshipped Zeus as their "God" supreme, how do Christians today differ in their worshipping?" Any question that Darden could put before them was intended to make them think, and they might conclude that for the Greeks and for the Christians, their religions were their beliefs, *if* they had any beliefs.

I remember that Darden and Marshall agreed on a definition for beliefs. "Beliefs are the habitual things in the mind that hold one's confidence in something," was how they put it. To me their account was a bit confusing. But, since the two agreed, I wasn't gonna say they were not thinking wisely.

Darden seemed able to talk in depth with Dee and Marshall by always questioning their explanations of myth. He would tell them his version, that myth represented repeated social occurrences or maybe just patterns which seemed to produce a towering and powerful body of gods.

The gods he referred to included not only Zeus, but Hades, Poseidon, Hera, Athene, and Ares. I don't recall reading enough to remember names of any lesser gods. But I do remember there was more than one level of Greek gods.

Dee must have impressed Marshall that I was particularly fascinated with the world of Hades, as whenever we had Greek mythology discussions, after Darden's death especially, I would catch Marshall reading me with a puzzled look on his face. One day when Dee and I were alone, I did ask her if she and Marshall ever talked about me. She said they did.

At their home, Dee told Marshall, "Ms. Leanna is always eager to talk about what she calls the duties of only two of the gods, Hades and Zeus."

"What exactly does she say, and when does she say whatever to you?"

"You've noticed she always invites me to come help her in the kitchen to prepare the tea and cookies? Well, that's when we seem to tarry while she heats the tea water on the back burner on medium low."

"So, what kind of things does she say?"

"Today she talked about Hades owning, and that's exactly what she said, owning, first Lethe and Mnemosyne, those two beautiful rivers that surrounded his palace just outside Tartarus. Ms. Leanna wondered what it might feel like to be able to regain one's lost memory. Her mood was much too deep for my head, today."

"But that's Ms. Leanna," Marshall said. "I think she is really cool. She knows a bunch, and she comes off as slightly less intelligent than those of us who have completed college. I really like her. She's just real cool."

Dee confessed that she told Marshall she secretly worried about me having such deep concern about the two rivers Lethe and Mnemosyne that flowed in the underground region of Tartarus governed by the Greek god Hades.

I was extremely happy when Dee and Marshall moved into the vacant house two houses diagonally across the street from me. This was now three years after Darden's death, and one year after Racina moved into my home, *uninvited*. Those two young people had joined the huge turnout for Darden's funeral and wept as openly as our own children and other family members. They continued their visits with me and I was determined to be the gracious hostess they accused me of being.

Dee, now a member of my neighborhood community group, became a seeing-eye neighborhood witness now that she was no longer employed outside the home. But, her witnessing and telling news was for Marshall's ears only. Her witnessing was both in close and from afar.

From her house diagonally down across the street, Dee saw who came to visit with me and how long they stayed; and, during any visits she herself paid me she knew exactly which of my children or grand-children came and what each child did for me, to me, and about me.

"Hi, Ms. Leanna. It's me, Dee. Would you like some company? I thought I'd stop in for a visit and hoped you would feel like sitting on your porch today."

"Sure, Honey, come on up. Let me get my sweater and I'll join you on the porch. I feel like rocking for a bit."

Dee had been in my company many times and seemed to enjoy the flashbacks to my early childhood that most always accompanied my porch rocking. I kinda think that's why she often suggested that we sit on the porch for our visits. I secretly think that Dee's close resemblance to her grandma Amelia likewise triggered some of those flashbacks.

"Amy, did your baby sleep alright after you gave her her medicine?" Dee thought I was talking to myself if I answered such questions, but I was merely trying to relate exactly how we had played so well together back when her grandma and I were children. "Oh, no, dear, I didn't have to do anything last night. Missy was so tuckered out, she just went right to sleep."

And on it went in that flavor for many of Dee's visits.

I never thought that Dee was visiting out of idle curiosity. Instead, I felt there was a real fondness for me even before Darden died, and it seemed an even deeper fondness now. Thus, my rambling in and out of those flashbacks, which caused some occasional inattention to my guest, in no way put off Dee. She understood that some of the rambling may be due to my advanced age or maybe only to mild dementia. She never made such a statement to me, but since I had some experience at reading facial expressions, I thought she might have some such opinions.

Many of the activities away from home that I had often participated in had long ago ceased to be. I didn't feel I was that lucid, often enough, to continue with the church youth cooking classes, nor even the Bible verse discussion classes with the church youth.

Though Braxton did not live right here in Graybar, he frequented sports events that were held here. And when he was in town for some sports event, he would stop by the house for a visit. Now, trust me, Braxton had picked up one nasty attitude, was an unpretentious drunk, and took out his frustrations with everything all on me.

Several times Dee had come over during Braxton's visits and saw and heard him abusing me. "Hey, ol' lady, you sure look like crap today. What's with that outfit—green, red, blue, purple, brown? If you can't do any better than that, you oughta stop trying. Ha! Ha!" He reeked of whiskey-born sourness on such days, but that shouldn't have given him an excuse to verbally abuse me.

Dee told Marshall that apparently Braxton was so unforgiving that he was still looking for someone to blame for Larson's horrible murder. "Ms. Leanna is the person he was next most fond of, so he takes his anger out on her. One day I actually saw Mr. Braxton purposely push her down, but she fell upon the sofa. She must not have been hurt, but I wasn't gonna leave her alone with her own son."

"So, does that mean you did some interfering into their lives that day?"

"I did, but not in the way you think."

"Do tell. Just what way was it that you interfered?"

"I told Mr. Braxton that just shortly before he arrived, his mother and I were getting ready to go to the grocery store, and I asked him if there was anything we could bring back for him. That was the way I interfered, and I hoped to God Almighty that Ms. Leanna was sharp enough to dig what I was up to."

"Yeah, honey, you love those pecan whirleys so much I'll bring back a package for you. You will be here when we get back, won't you?"

"Marshall, Ms. Leanna caught on and responded brilliantly, then disappeared down the hall and returned wearing a blue sweater and saying, "Are you ready now, Dee?"

"Yes, Ma'am, I'm ready. We can go, now?"

En route to the store, Ms. Leanna confided in me, "I thought I understood my children, but I guess I still have a lot to learn."

"I'm not sure what you are referring to, Ms. Leanna."

She replied, "You just witnessed my remaining son raise his hand in violence to me. Me, *his mother*! I don't ever remember having to give him a switching while he was growing from boy to man. What could be his problem? What could I have done to him that caused him to turn on me?"

"Ms. Leanna, since I'm the outsider, I don't think I should even voice an opinion. Are you sure you don't have any idea what could be going on with Mr. Braxton?"

After a quiet moment or two, Ms. Leanna spoke up and was revealing something totally different. "Dee, do you know how to sew?"

"Yes, Ma'am. My major in college was Home Economics. Of course, I'll bet what I learned formally in school in no way equals your sewing skills. I've heard all about the many things you've sewn on sewing machines, and the many crafts you have created with the knitting needles and tatting needles too."

"Oh, child, who told you that?" I know I blushed.

All that young lady did was drive us here and there, and before long I had risen up and out of my depressed state into a touch of happiness as I was buying a goodie for my son. We stopped at a grocery store, found and bought the pecan whirleys and just a few other things before we returned home. I guess we had tried Braxton's patience and won. He had left the house.

The attention that Dee was giving me was a tremendous relief for Racina who now had frequent opportunities to relax, maybe get her hair done at the beauty parlor, and even go to a movie. Dee had asked no one for pay, and wouldn't have accepted were it offered. She paid attention to me out of sheer fondness for me. That I now knew.

During a visit with Dee, maybe about seven or so years after Darden's death, I was eagerly diving into a discussion about Greek myths. I do know that we, no, I talked a lot about the god Hades, but I asked Dee to tell me about the kinds of things that Hades did. She talked about the flower fields in Tartarus, the down under land, and about the rivers flowing there that were difficult to cross. It was that good discussion that keyed me into high spirits. Suddenly I heard the music in my head. I found myself having such a brilliant discussion with Dee about the Greek myths that I interrupted our conversation with a soprano outburst of the hymn "Be Still, My Soul."

"Ms. Leanna, are you alright?" Her look upon my face and the strange nervousness of her question brought me abruptly back to the present time. Dee made a quick excuse, that she forgot she promised Marshall a special meal, so she had to rush home to get it cooked by the time of his arrival.

"Okay, honey. I can't thank you enough for all the time you spend with me. I so enjoy our talks."

She voiced, "You're most welcome, Ms. Leanna. Bye for now." I saw a tear land near my sofa as she whirled and went out the front door.

Some days later when next we met, Dee suggested that I seemed depressed and that she understood how the death of Mr. Darden, followed by the deaths of my son Larson, and my daughter Neva, all so close together, could cause symptoms of depression. And though she would not speak it, I'm sure she was including the harsh mental and physical treatments that my children were putting me through, as the causes of those depressing symptoms. Such a wise child to perceive the turnabout of 360 degrees by my family in dealing with me, their old and ancient mother.

My children had been real sweethearts, honorable and respectful in every way toward me. But that was then, and this is now. They yell at me when I do something they don't like, or tell about something that they believe never took place. And more than a few times, I've been physically steered down the hall to the bath and gotten my face and hands scrubbed. All of them act ashamed of what I have aged into. Like hearing me repeat an event more than just a few times all in the same discussion period is disgusting to them. Or, perhaps I might dress myself a second time in the same hour but hear neither approval nor disapproval of my dress choices.

I overheard bits of a conversation between Dee and Marshall one day when she voiced, "Forever, I'll be a friend to Ms. Leanna. Forever, I say."

CHAPTER 11

▼

LOSING THE BATTLE

I wish I could figure out if something is bothering me. It has to be something big. Big, because my rocking on the front porch won't bring up many thoughts about my yesteryears in Cayuga like it used to. Of course, I have reached my ninety-sixth year so that fact alone could be causing me this stress.

Also, the association with my children and the raw attitudes they take about me doing anything—housework, gardening, or other yard-work—has driven me to the point where I just throw up my hands and let them do as they darned well please. Anytime I look for something in my linen closet, I know the shelves are left in disarray. I don't mind looking at what I do, neat or messy. But, at least one of my children is gonna scold me. "Mother, why do you always do that? I had that closet all straightened out, and now you've messed it up. Again!"

"Well, it is *my* house, you know!" I've begun to wonder if my children will ever sing a different tune to me, especially about my linen closet, because I declare they started that tune all of a century ago.

"But that doesn't mean you should go around messing up what we've just straightened up for you, Mama."

"Did I ask you to straighten it up, for me, in the first place?" I didn't bother to try to control my anger at any one of my children or grandchildren. I felt that the frequency of their visits now and the hustle and bustle of their activities in my home over these past years had besieged me as a plague. Yes, a plague!

"Oh, Mother!" accompanied by a stamped foot was usually their disgusted reply. But then the complainer would set about correcting the thing that we had just disagreed on.

I mused about how long my children were going to contradict my every word. Their opposition to my truths began about the same time as had their complaints about my linen closet.

Once upon a time I did think that I could best my children on anything they challenged me with, but I never thought I'd have to deal with the grandchildren in the very same manner. Well, if I started to reveal a conversation I had with a friend, any of them would disagree with me, stating, "Oh, Mom, that isn't what was said." Or, "Nana, are you sure you were talking with her?"

It was but a few years back, when Braxton stopped in he greeted me with a pleasant, "Hi, Mom."

I always replied, "Hi, honey."

"I came by to see how you are doing. What'cha been up to?" Or, "Been doing anything exciting, lately?"

I nearly stated, "Surely you can't believe that getting out of bed and going to a different room just to sit is exciting." I held my tongue when it dawned on me he didn't come around often enough to observe my daily routines, none of which were ever exciting. Instead, I would say, "Not really. You know me. What is there to get excited about?"

Braxton kept up Larson's pastime of sending me potted plants or cut flowers for any occasion that he thought of. I did a great job, I thought, of caring for the flowers. But Braxton closely examined every flower he sent or brought and forever found fault with the care I gave.

"Mom, what happened to that astilbe?"

"What's an astilbe, honey? Oh, you mean that plant I set out by the east corner of the back stoop? I watered it just like I was told. What do you mean, what's happened with it?"

"Well, just come on outside and look at it." We went out the front door and around to the east side of the house when he asked, "Doesn't it look sick to you?"

"Well, let me tell you this, honey." I slapped my hands on my hips and set my right foot some inches apart from my left foot, cocked my head upward at a right angle and looked down my left cheek at his stooped figure. "When I set something out here in God's little acre, all that I can't do for that something, God surely will. *That* plant's gonna be all right!"

"Yeah, right. What I see is you still kill every flower that you get. I don't know why I bother bringing them."

"I guess I don't know either."

I went back into the house via the kitchen and went down the hall to my bedroom, closed the door, stuck my fingers in my ears, then sat down on the side of the bed. In some fifteen minutes or so I came out of the room and Braxton had left my house.

Braxton's whole demeanor has drastically changed since Larson's death. He was no longer close with his younger sisters. Of course they spoke and even got together occasionally, but each knew that their special something was now missing. And with me he had become rather brash.

On one of his visits, Racina had prepared a pot of tea and put it on the table for me to pour my own cup when I was ready. Braxton seized the opportunity to be hateful.

"Oh, gimme the pot, Mom, I'll pour the tea for you. I don't know why Racina didn't pour the stuff in the kitchen." He seemed to be chiding me and Racina simultaneously, but only I was within earshot. "Should you be drinking tea, Mom?"

"No one has ever told me I shouldn't. Why would you think that?"

"They usually take the good stuff from all old folks. And you're old folks now. Ha, ha."

I fired a quick question on a different subject to stiffle *any* further hostility welling up in his innards. "Where are the children, Brax? Didn't anyone come with you?"

"I left everybody back home. Half the time I feel like I'm being strangled when they are around. I needed some free time away from them." He was standing above me looking menacingly at me. "What do you care where they are? I know they get on your nerves. Anyway, I left everybody just fine." He mellowed somewhat after he had a moment to reflect on the question I had just asked. It appeared he might be feeling a twinge of regret about the way he was acting. He was sober that day. He sat in the chair across from me.

Very seldom did Edril's widow, Darcy, or any of their children stop in to visit, though they lived near enough to Graybar to come often. They knew the way to my home; usually, Darcy had tagged along with Edril. All of us knew that Darcy was a domineering personality, but we all gave her credit for confining it to within her own household. Yet I didn't look upon Darcy's absence as disrespect. I did think that Edril's children should pay me a visit now and then. "Oh well, maybe I don't want to contend with their insults, either."

My life now consists of bickering, bickering, and more bickering, with any of my children or grandchildren who do come by to check on whether I am "all right." Any one of the faces represents a hostile invasion. I am so tired of the hassles. So very tired.

I guess I had been sitting and staring at that floor, unseeing, for a long while when I remembered that Maida, who lived a thousand miles away, would be passing through town on Monday en route to her job in the southeast. I surely wanted to be home that day. Whenever we get to see each other, we have such pleasant visits. Maida's job was as Finalizer on Claims for a large insurance company.

You know, perhaps Maida is the only child who understands the lasting effects any death can have on an individual. She, herself, has voiced how devastated she still feels over the loss of her father. A death followed so closely by the loss of two of her siblings. Also, I think it was a few years back when Maida grasped the reality of several situations involving me, and concluded that all that fussing after me was depressing me, so she avoided fussing with me about anything. She decided that now was the right time to be my best friend. You can call it reciprocation for when she was young. Golly, how I appreciated that. Monday came, and so did Maida. We had a very pleasant visit.

We talked of general things as the weather, and how each had fared during the particular season. From that we moved on to chatter about how much weight one of us had gained and the other one lost. We continued with a discussion on Maida's inability to bake decent pies because she made awful pie crusts. I suggested, "Well, honey, why don't you just buy those frozen pie crusts, and build your pie from that?"

"Gosh, Mom, why didn't I think of that? How many times have I seen those crusts in the store, yet not focused on what they were to be used for? Silly of me, I know." We had deep hearty laughs about that.

Our visit this time ended same as most of the other visits, "I love you, Mother. You know that."

"I love you, too, honey."

By now you ought to know that "honey" is the name that I use for each one of my children when I can't readily remember his or her name. Lately, seems only "honey" or "child" are the names that come to my mind. And just the other day when one of the youth from the church, to whom I had taught cooking, stopped for a visit, I even called her "honey." She wore a mild smile during that whole visit. I suspect she was pleased with my name for her.

I put on my pale pink sweat suit and white tennis shoes and sat on the back stoop and was watching my grandson go through his usual ritual of pretending to be working hard at mowing and raking my lawn. I would mow my own lawn, but these children won't even let me exercise my legs by walking behind my mower, not even for five minutes. The work is not that difficult, it's just that Bradley is disgruntled at having been sent over here by his father to do the job.

Let me tell you how this child's mind works. Bradley walks a few paces behind the mower, spots a twig he figures is too big to be chopped by the mower, stops the mower, goes around in front of it and removes the twig by tossing it in a direction that he has not yet covered, then proceeds to mow some more. Once he reaches that same twig, again he stops the mower, goes around in front of it, picks up the twig and tosses it in yet another direction he has not yet mowed.

I was thoroughly amused watching him. At first. But then I wondered just how long the child was going to follow the same routine before he realized it would be to his advantage to select an already mowed area to toss that twig or stack the several twigs he kept encountering. His other grandmother once told me, "Bradley is a very smart child."

And I wondered, "Gee, how could she know?" To my own private thoughts I laughed out loud.

Soon, I tired of watching his foolishness and left the back stoop. I chose to sit in my favorite gold chair firmly planted by the open front door where I watched the people as they rode the bus, drove a car, or walked past my home.

I was in a hurry to get out of bed this morning. I'm still wondering why. Anyway, I put on my pink and white robe and tucked it into my black leggings. My white sox matched my outfit perfectly. Racina said I had to change my clothes, but I liked what I had on. She grabbed me by the arm and pulled me down the hall to my bedroom and ordered me to put on the clothes she chose for me.

I said to that Racina child, "Now, you have just gone too far. Certainly, you haven't gotten too big for your britches that you think you can make me change, I'm sure."

She didn't answer me with words. She pulled the robe up out of my leggings and bent my arms back pulling off the thing. In its place she pulled on a pink blouse. After she pushed me down on the bed, she pulled off the shoes, sox, and leggings I had on and pulled on some grey cotton long pants instead, before replacing the white sox and my sneaker shoes.

This "properly" dressing me was a ritual begun by Racina every day just before she dropped me off at Pectola's home, where I was to stay until Racina was off work and picked me up later in the day. This ritual was a heavy, heavy burden and it caused me to imagine myself the one working, getting up early every morning, getting dressed, and going to my job—to babysit. Racina did explain the change from me staying at home and being visited by Dee to now being dropped off at Pecky's house. She said Dee had accepted a job as plant manager at the new textile factory. This change is absolute proof that I have lost all opportunity to be free, free like my sisters and brothers were free.

True that Pecky and I are friends from years ago, but we aren't finding anything in common to talk about now. I don't even want to sit still. I can't eat. I am not finding any reasons to smile. But I've assured Pecky that she is not the cause. I think she understands.

Maida was planning her retirement for November and was hoping to visit me more often. Locally, when she was not searching for a suitable property to purchase for relocating her family, she would stop for a visit with me and Pectola at Pecky's home. One of those times, I had refused to eat the lunch prepared by Racina, so Maida treated me and Pecky out to lunch. She took us to a hotdog stand and purchased "full up" dogs—two for each of us. We sat at a roadside table and thoroughly enjoyed every crumb that had been placed before us.

"Such fun," I told Maida and Pectola. "No problems, no cares, no one telling me what to do or when to do it. This is really great fun."

Another time Maida invited us, me and Pectola, out with her to the bowling alley where she was meeting some of her own long-time friends. I surprised myself when I perked up my footsteps, frisked about, was smiling and greeting everyone. I even called one person by her real name, though it was about twenty years since I last saw her.

The moments were brief, but I felt I was testing my memory, and thinking, "Yes, I do. I still have all of my faculties!"

Maida's facial expression showed she was cooking up something. She promised her friends that when she could meet with them again that she would bring Mrs. Nedley, you know that's Pectola, and me along. She said she would alert them in time for them to also bring an elderly guest who might want to bowl. The opportunity arrived, Maida contacted her friends, and the stage was set. Or was it?

I learned at a much later time that Maida had phoned the house to speak with me but reached only Racina who told her, after about twenty minutes of conversation, that I was not home.

"She's not here. She and Cordice left last Monday going up to Cordice's."

"Well, when is she coming home?"

"When she feels like it," Racina arrogantly stated.

During Maida's revelation to me about that particular incident, she said she abruptly hung up because she was stunned and deeply hurt that she was the last to know that I was not going to be home for awhile. After some moments of regaining some composure, Maida redialed the house and asked Racina what had provoked the last phone scenario.

"You have to figure that one out for yourself," was Racina's reply.

"Racina! That is my mother, too, and I have a right to know everything you know, and when you know it, if it's about Mother." Maida hung up the phone feeling that she had good reason to be angry with Racina.

I have always been aware of the differences in the personalities of my girls. Racina and Cordice were the "hotheads" in the family, that is, they were determined to have situations always go their way. Neva was a "fence" straddler, meaning she sometimes sided with Racina and Cordice against Maida, and other times not with them against anyone.

Cordice was more secretive about what she was up to than was Racina, which kept Cordice out of the spotlight as the culprit in whatever the situation. Racina, on the other hand, delighted in letting everyone and anyone know how she could get inside Maida's head.

Early on, I didn't see this "wrangling" as hatred nor even jealousy toward Maida, but instead, real curiosity followed by immediate and impromptu responses from Maida, no matter what situations Racina, Cordice, or Neva presented. They seemed thrilled.

Racina was about eighteen months old when she began pestering Maida by insisting that she immediately locate a favorite toy that she had "lost." Or when Maida was settled in a chair and reading a book, Racina would call to Cordice and the two of them would insist that Maida read aloud to them. Maybe Maida was taking a bath when Racina and Cordice insisted they needed to use the bathroom. Right now! Maida hated for them to ask her direct questions about why certain of their body parts were not the same size, or for them to giggle and point at her body asking why she had hair growth where they had none, or other such questions. Maida found it very difficult to be harsh or scolding with them being that she was much older than they, so she always called on me to put an end to such occurrences.

Maida's personality resembled my own, passive. I know now, but not back then, that I favored Maida more than my other daughters, but that was never my intentions, ever.

Throughout my children's young years, I was the mediator, the judge, and the jury in settling whatever their problems. I escaped that kind of mental stress all of their adult years, that is, until now when I sense animosity between Racina, Cordice, and Maida. I thank God for such relief.

I'm having a flashback and it's about how much fun I used to have when I visited the homes of my children. The children used to cram their days and weekends with mall shopping trips, dinners at elaborate restaurants, Sunday and Wednesday church services, front porch evening talks about our yesteryears, and public park outings where we purchased truck-vended hotdogs and hamburgers overflowing with hot onions, sauerkraut, and meat sauce.

This visit at Cordice's home is so different, perhaps because it is not of my free will. Cordice and Racina had slightly warmed conversations about the "free" time Cordice enjoyed while Racina had none. Cordice had no job outside the home. There was only herself, her husband, and anyone's children she might agree to tolerate for a few hours, occasionally. So to even up the "free" time slots, Racina handed me off to Cordice for an undisclosed period of time. The first nine weeks of my visit, which lasted all of four months, were joyful weeks for me, really. Joyful because I was privileged to do things. Many of these things happened in Cordice's kitchen.

"Mother, I can use your help in the kitchen. I'm running late getting dinner prepared. Would you stir this milk into the cornbread mix, then pour it into that pan?"

"Sure, honey, I'll just wash my hands first." I flashed a grin that stretched from my left ear to my right ear.

Trust me now, but not having done any work in anyone's kitchen for so long, I was beating instead of stirring, but Cordice made no comment. That first time she really was late getting dinner started. She even asked me to do yet another task.

"Now, Mom, if you will, use those plates there and set the table for dinner. Eddie will be here in a few minutes as hungry as a grizzly bear."

"Honey, what's a grizzly bear?"

"Oh, you remember what a bear looks like. We saw Gentle Ben on TV just last night."

"Oh, yeah. Now I remember."

At Cordice's, the kitchen tasks got to be regular happenings for me, and that made me disbelieve my own senses. Let me explain. Cordice is so accommodating here, but not when she's at my house. I don't understand what is going on.

After a few days of my helping in the kitchen routines, I sought to have a chat with Cordice for some clarification of this change.

"Cordice, how come you let me do these things in your house, but I can't do these same things in my house?"

"Is that how you see things? Well, this is my house and I do as I choose. At your house, I try to appease Racina who said she had everything well established."

"Oh, I guess so." Suddenly, I was unable to focus through a cloud of mental confusion. That verbal exchange was ended. After I gave several quick jolts to the side of my head with a palm-heel bang twice, I was still confused, but the cloud was brightening. I aimed to keep talking.

"Cordice, can we go to the park one day soon?"

Cordice chuckled, then said, "You always did like the swings at the park. Sure, I think we can do that tomorrow."

"Can you still buy hotdogs off the truck like we used to do?"

"No, Mom. People became careless about discarding their trash in the designated receptacles which prompted the officers of the Park Commission to institute a law disallowing foods in the parks. People can use only the provided play equipment. Tossing of missiles such as balls or Frisbees is to be done in the posted specified areas, or the offending persons lose their properties."

"I don't know if I want to swing anymore, so let's don't go to the park."

"Okay."

I was asked to do a job not in the kitchen—sweep the front and back porches. That is, until the day that I accidentally knocked over the flower pot that held the peach-colored African violet. Cordice went past furious. She acted as though she had a sudden PMS attack.

"Confound it, Mother. Look what you've done! That was my most prized flower because of its color. It's so delicate that I doubt that I can salvage anything; it's all crushed. How could you be so clumsy?" My child was yelling loud enough to be heard half a block away.

And yes, something must have snapped in me because my temper also flared. I threw the broom down and walked off the porch heading north away from the house. Cordice stood there watching me while mouthing off that she wished I was someplace other than at her house.

I had reached the end of the block before Cordice got in her car and drove up alongside me, then stopped.

"Get in the car, Mother."

"I don't have to do that. No, I don't."

"Get in the car, Mother. Now!"

Cordice was yelling so loud now that I stopped and just stared straight ahead. To help my balance, I folded my left arm across my waist, put my right hand on my hip, and shifted all my weight to my left leg. I must have stood like that for all of five minutes before Cordice got out of her car. Gently, she took me by the arm, and nudged me over to and into her car. You know, before that very moment, I had not realized that I was in a contest to prove who could best the other.

From that day on, Cordice refused to allow me to help her with anything. I would now witness that Cordice was really stressed, much, much more than when she was finding simple things for me to do. Oh, no, Cordice did not like that. Absolutely no one must stress Cordice!

I no longer got the slightest tug at being comfortable now, not after that last encounter with Cordice. Something kept tugging at me, though, and before long I thought I knew what it was. I vaguely recalled Maida saying she was going to take me bowling again, but if I'm correct that was a very long time ago. Wonder why she hasn't called me? That's not like her at all! Why won't Maida come for me?

Finally, after being at Cordice's for four months, I got sent home. It was exactly one week after Cordice called Racina and told her she had had enough of my stubbornness, and that Racina could just resume her job of looking after me. Racina, during that phone conversation, reminded Cordice, "As long as I have my own good health, Mother will not become a resident in any nursing home."

A brief memory breakthrough allowed me to understand that Racina meant every word of what she spoke, but I could see that she tired quickly at doing the job she had assured her siblings she would do, all those years ago.

I tried to be obedient at what I had come to understand were Racina's desires for me. I spent my days sitting, staring and not seeing, and guessing at why Maida would not come for me and Pectola. It was a very long time since Maida had contacted me.

"Racina, would you telephone Maida and find out when she will be coming to take me bowling again?"

Racina was entering her bedroom as she answered me. "Yes, Mom, I'll call her."

I didn't know it at that moment but it was obvious days later, that Racina had only been pretending to be talking on the telephone. The notion to try to eavesdrop had never entered my head, so there was no way for me to prove if she was or was not speaking to Maida. Shortly, Racina returned to the livingroom where we had begun our conversation.

This is what she told me. "Maida said she was called to work on short notice after a co-worker became ill right in the middle of a company closure transaction. She really doesn't know how long it's going to take to end that case."

"Well, did she say she would call me?"

"No ma'am."

"Hm, that's strange."

It was about the time that Maida was first hired on her job and got to travel extensively, that I noticed the tension that flared between Cordice, Racina, and Maida. I've always known that between Cordice and Racina, those two could start a nothing avalanche with only half of nothing available! Jealousy exists among these three! Or rather, Cordice and Racina are jealous of Maida. But why?

No, no, it ought not to be about Maida's traveling. She is the last of my children to even afford a trip almost next door to the beach, while

Cordice, Racina, and all of the other children did a good deal of traveling soon after each was married.

"Oh, my gosh! That's it, they won't let Maida know where I am! Well, well, well. Can you beat that? My grown children still toying with Maida's mind!" I need to be saying this only to myself.

The children continued to taunt Maida by refusing to answer any of her questions, or to offer her any information about my general welfare. It was this painful, emotional onslaught on her that caused her to retreat within herself and away from her siblings. I guessed that she was trying hard not to be the one causing me any anguish.

Maida reasoned that her siblings had somehow been misguided about treatment for my current stage of forgetfulness, and that they intentionally excluded her as a family member with a right to know all that they knew. Maida further reasoned that Racina was feeling heavily burdened because she had no social life since losing all of her friends after her divorce. She saw other things that had to be working against Racina: Cordice scheduled less time for visiting; Braxton became a work horse with no free time; the grandchildren, especially those living in or near Graybar, all found reasons not to be there frequently to relieve Racina even for a moment or two.

One of those Graybar community groups, especially the nosy neighborhood one, was now viewing my children's behavior toward me as ungrateful and uncaring.

I reasoned mentally, "Surely, just because the paternal glue is gone is no reason for this family to fall apart. I am here, your maternal glue. Where's your respect for me?"

CHAPTER 12

▼

SHUTDOWN

Because I forget so many things so frequently these days, I think my children believe that I can't hear, at least, not well anyway. If we're in the same room space, they will speak in normal tones to each other when discussing the feasibility of having me confined in one of those special places where I've heard others are put when they no longer do things the way the relatives or guardians want them done.

Not even I believed anyone could ever feel so tired. But these days, right now, that is how I feel—tired, tired, tired. I think I'm doing the same type of exercises that I've always done, but maybe not. I haven't jumped rope with any young people in quite a while. Have I? Gosh, something is not the same.

Several years ago, I and a few of my peers visited several places called nursing homes where some of our long time friends had been left because no relative could or would give them the care they needed.

There are some peers I once fraternized with who are still on their own. So, why don't they come around anymore? But never you mind, I'll be just fine once my young friends stop by. Their visits seem to allow me many moments of rationality.

I'm getting upset way too often now. Maida was here late in the afternoon and was questioning me.

"Mama, where in the world have you been all the week? I've been calling and getting no answer. Just what have you been up to?"

I bristled, clinched my fists, and squinted my eyes before I answered as I didn't know if her tone was scolding me or if she was naturally curious.

"They were having revival at our church, and you knew I was gonna be there. On Thursday night I had a terrible headache, so I took some medicine."

"Mama, you didn't take any medicine," chimed Racina into Maida's and my conversation.

"I know I did take some medicine!" I knew that I had just been upstaged.

Racina directed the next words to Maida, "Mama didn't take any medicine; she doesn't have to take any medicine."

"For my headache, Pectola did give me two Bufferin and I took them. I know what I'm talking about."

I'd had it with Racina, so I got up from my chair, tossed my head up in the air, plodded down the hall to my bedroom, and plopped down in my favorite chair. For the moment I could only heave a heavy sigh, for relief. Once was not enough to get out all the anger I was feeling, so I heaved yet another heavy sigh, then stared straight ahead at my mind's vision of Racina who was perched on an arm of the sofa in the living room.

I could hear the shouting exchange of words between Maida and Racina.

"Racina, do you think correcting Mother's every word is the thing to do to her at her age?"

"Oh, you just shut up, Missy, you don't live here, so you don't know what's going on."

"Then, why don't you answer me when I ask of you what's going on?"

"Ha, because I don't have to. Oh, you make me sick. You know too damn much now."

"I see, we're back to the same old hang-up. You think that I think I'm so important just because I have a college degree and you don't. Is that your problem?"

"Well, you said it, I didn't."

"But, that is what you think, right?"

"Yeah, that's what I think."

"In case you have forgotten, you had the same opportunity as I did to attend college. Only you got hooked on your man, got married, and forgot about educating yourself barely beyond high school. You did just what you wanted to do. So don't take out your frustration on me. I'm the least of whom you should blame. After all these years of suffering indignities at the hands of your mate, you have the nerve to blame me for your problems. I learned a long time ago, that when you make your bed hard, you have to lie in it."

Immediately after that brave exhalation of words by Maida, she came into my room. She hugged me tightly, kissed me on the cheek, apologized for being the cause of my discomfort, and said she was leaving now, before it got dark. She said she had curtailed her night driving due to night blindness, but that she would be in touch, and soon.

Maida let me know that on more than one occasion, she had heard Braxton's browbeating contradictions, much like what she had witnessed from Racina.

Braxton's thing, a mimic of Larson's habit, was sending or bringing potted plants occasionally to me. If, on a visit, Braxton saw one wilted leaf, or felt the potting soil was too dry for the plant, he made an argument happen with me. The arguing was happening with such regularity that I couldn't carry on a conversation about anything to anyone.

Racina vented all of her frustrations on me now. I'm lucid enough to guess that Racina wants out of her current predicament, and away from me in particular. No one will sit with me even for an hour for her to have privacy with anyone.

Racina makes me pay for her predicament. All I hear now is a constant loud noise, some of you might call it music, but to my ears it is torturous *noise*. I try to stop the noise, but I get so confused when I reach over to turn the radio off. I don't know how to turn it off nor what to do, anymore. So, the music-noise just continues on hour after hour, day after day, year after year, just as it did throughout many of the years while I was married to Darden. The big difference—Darden had not been angry with anyone when he listened to the radio, and so as not to disturb *anyone*, Darden kept the radio volume at a low level until he was asked to increase it so others could also hear the music or whatever was the program.

I am aware that my children continue to invade my home, taking turns at doing all of the things that I have always done, and still want to do by myself, and for myself. Maybe I'm not capable of doing anything. Will I know again, ever? None of the children stay the night, nor on weekends to relieve Racina as she requests of them. My children also continue to annoy me by dissecting every word that I dare utter. They are trying to persuade me that they are giving me great care, the kind of care that I *need*. But, guess what? At this point in my life, their words only play leapfrog up and over my head.

The intensity of their "care" is so overwhelming that I'm literally helpless to offer further resistance to any of the children. I am not eating because I have no desire for food. Perhaps that's another reason why I'm so very tired, and maybe even why my hair is so dry and brittle. I'm not getting proper nutrition so maybe my body's chemistry is so whacked out is why I'm having to try three times harder at recognizing any child's face, and seldom, if ever, one's name.

Cordice and Braxton spent three hours here today, all the while claiming that I was upsetting them by deliberately refusing to do what they told me to do. The moment Racina arrived home from work, Cordice and Braxton left the house spouting, "I'm totally exasperated," in unison.

Racina, herself in a funky mood because her boss had required her to redo a project three times before he would accept it, started in on me with more complaints about my attitude.

"Old Lady, I don't care what the others say, I'm taking you to the Charene Functions Center. You can't stay here anymore. I'm too tired to mess with you when I get home. Since no one else wants to take care of you, I'm not going to do it anymore, either."

While I entertain pure rage at each one of my children, I choose to sit in my favorite gold chair positioned right near the front door. This fact I know, crossing my left leg high up on the thigh of my right leg sure does feel comfortable.

Goodness me, for what reason am I snapping my head from side to side? Gosh, now my head has dropped forward, I don't seem to be in control. Uh, oh, I can't focus my eyes. Now they're rolling back up into their sockets. I feel my eyelids slowly closing. Huh, I am not even feeling angry about the "care" that my children have chosen to give me. Gee whiz, now my stability seems so unbalanced. I am not hearing my music in my head, Lord, Lord. Oh, dear God, is it my time? I think that I am ready! Yes, Lord, I *am* ready!

With my last ounce of conscious strength, Lord, if I have a choice, I choose to simply shut down, completely.

Lethe!

CHAPTER 13

▼

SUMMARY

And that's how it happened. The maternal glue, Mother, Mom, Mama, Ms. Leanna, "the lovable dove," a very long way past her prime in life at the age of ninety-six, most certainly and successfully eluded her stalkers.

Will she be found? Will she return from Lethe? Her children, all of them, most surely arrogated her last available resources for life.

Leanna, the child, was totally unprivileged to use her own mind.

Leanna, the teenager, was married, and then was obligingly unprivileged to use her own mind.

Leanna, the widow, was overwhelmed by her "caregiving" children, and rendered unprivileged to use her own mind.

Yes, it happened. The maternal glue, Mother, Mom, Mama, Ms. Leanna, "the lovable dove," entered into the waters of Lethe.

Leanna Mallard Swelton, alone, is at the mercy of that Olympian god, Hades. Will Hades allow Mother, Mom, Mama, Ms. Leanna, "the lovable dove," whose name is written in the Book of Life, to wade into the waters of Mnemosyne?

Leanna Mallard Swelton, a lovable but elusive dove, aided by her memories into her past, finally knows who she is. Her decision has set her free!!

# # #

0-595-25824-7